ADVANCE PRAISE for
Women In Bed

"What we do – or don't or won't do – for love, in all its incarnations, is at the fiercely beating heart of this stellar collection of linked stories. As exhilarating as love at first sight, and written in prose as clear and spare as a single bed, these stories linger, haunt and showcase the talents of a literary master."

> – Caroline Leavitt, *New York Times*
> bestselling author of *Pictures of You*
> and *Is This Tomorrow*

"It is impossible to turn away from these beautiful and evocative stories. Jessica Keener explores the courage, vulnerabilities, and strength of women in every phase of life. No matter who you are, you will see a version of yourself illuminated in this poignant, powerful book."

> – Jessica Anya Blau, author of
> *The Wonder Bread Summer*

"Seductive, incandescent, suspenseful, and wise, Women in Bed is a masterful collection that explores a landscape of intimate love, heartbreak, and desire. Keener's writing has a thrilling clarity. At once multifaceted and seamless, these stories map, with searing precision, the intricacies of the heart and those irrevocable moments on which a life turns."

> – Dawn Tripp, author of *Game of Secrets* and
> winner of the Massachusetts Book Award

Praise for Jessica Keener's novel
Night Swim

"Like the adults in Rick Moody's *Ice Storm*, the central couple in this novel of 1970s suburbia are remote alcoholics. 'Love was something distant that retired to a room on the second floor,' Sarah, the 16-year-old narrator, says, referring to her stay-at-home yet absentee mother. This is a woman who makes a divot in the soil for her drink glass while tending her roses ... This earnest debut centers on Sarah as she tunnels through new depths of loneliness ... moving."

— The New York Times

"Keener's observations perfectly capture a certain kind of 1970s adolescence: the adults who tried too hard, the sudden appearance of a joint when in the presence of older cousins, the way a grownup party could spin from fun to disturbing in a blink. Most exhilaratingly, she taps into the thrilling moments when a girl of 16 can see her future, whether in music or books or a boy's smile. Sarah watches her mother's rose garden after her death. Like her children, some 'bloomed haphazardly while some wilted,' a living symbol of what goes on, no matter what."

— The Boston Globe

"Rooted in personal sorrow, this memorable debut will strike a universal chord with readers: 'Life was full of befores and afters.'"

— Booklist

"Keener understands deeply that scene writing creates powerful moments for her characters. We learn of Sarah's irritation, fear, reticence, and desire not through discussion, but through her actions and interactions with others. And Keener's writing is lovely; she manages to build sentences that are both precise and ornate. While Keener's *Night Swim* tells of a girl who has lost her bearings, her hold on her novel is both assured and poised."
– Jewish Book Council

"Jessica Keener's debut novel *Night Swim* is a masterfully told tale. Dysfunctional family dynamics are revealed in language evocative and honest, and her characters so well drawn they could be our own kin. The emotional depth of this novel has me constantly recommending it to friends in book clubs."
– Large-Hearted Boy

"This gripping first novel announces the arrival of a strong, distinct and fully evolved new voice."
– Jennifer Egan, Pulitzer Prize winner, and author of *A Visit from the Goon Squad*

"An amazing new literary voice, Jessica Keener explores the fine-laced network of tangled familial relations in language both bold and intricate. *Night Swim* is the deeply moving and devastatingly beautiful work of a fearless writer."
– Sara Gruen, *New York Times* bestselling author of *Water for Elephants*

"Jessica Keener has an ear for the nuances of family life and manages, in this book, a small miracle – describing, convincingly, a family suffering the rigidity and opaqueness of a small-scale tyrant, yet honoring his authority

and treating his painful struggles with kindness. Keener's heroine, a 16-year-old girl impatient to achieve womanliness, is a marvel of curiosity, impulsiveness, and generosity. What a lovely book!"
    – C. Michael Curtis, Fiction Editor, *The Atlantic*

"Reading this was pure pleasure. Just gorgeous. Jessica Keener's *Night Swim* is a poignant and sensual examination of a life and a nation on the cusp of change. Sixteen-year-old Sarah brings us a moody and burgeoning wisdom as she pulls us toward secrets we recognize – the desire to hurry past pain and loss toward adulthood, the pull to belong and yet not be absorbed completely into the will of others. In a delicate balance of rebellion and compassion, Sarah teaches us to listen and hold tight to our dreams."
    – Susan Henderson, author of *Up From the Blue*,
    A Shelf Awareness top 10 pick for 2010

Women in Bed

NINE STORIES BY

JESSICA KEENER

THE
STORY PLANT

The Story Plant
Studio Digital CT, LLC
PO Box 4331
Stamford, CT 06907

Copyright © 2013 by Jessica Keener
Jacket design by Barbara Aronica-Buck

Print ISBN-13: 978-1-61188-075-5
E-book ISBN-13: 978-1-61188-076-2

Visit our website at www.thestoryplant.com
Visit the author's website at www.jessicakeener.com

"Secrets" originally published in *Sundog: Southeast Review*; "Recovery" originally published in *The Chariton Review*, *Redbook* Second Prize winner; listed in *The Pushcart Prize* anthology under "Outstanding Writers"; "Papier-mâché" originally published in *Oktoberfest*, finalist award; "Boarders" originally published in *Heat City Review*; "Woman With Birds in Her Chest" originally published in *Elixir*; "Shoreline" originally published in *Northeast Corridor*, *Pushcart Prize* nominee; "Bird of Grief" originally published in *Connotation Press: An Online Artifact,* feature story of the month. "Forgiveness" originally published in *Santa Fe Literary Review*; "Heart" originally published in *Connotation Press: An Online Artifact*.

First Story Plant Paperback Printing: October 2013
Printed in the United States of America

For Barr

Contents

Acknowledgments

As a young writer, I had the good fortune of studying with the inimitable John Hawkes and Robert Coover, my teachers at Brown University. I thank them both for their guidance and for their celebration of the short story as something transformative and enduring. Thanks also to editors Jim Barnes, Ken Robidoux, Meg Tuite, and Timothy Gager who embraced and published many of these stories. With gratitude to: the ever-entrepreneurial Lou Aronica, and book design master, Barb Aronica-Buck. For sensitive reading, thank you Leora Skolkin-Smith. To my dear friends Risa Miller, Joyce Walsh, Sherrie Crow, Susan Keith, you have graced me with your intelligence and support. For early encouragement, thank you C. Michael Curtis, Mitchell Kaplan, Steve Kronen, Laura Mullaney, Matty Bloom, Les Standiford, the Cava family, and Uncle Richard. Thank you Emma Sweeney and Noah Ballard.

I look back to the very beginning of things and thank my father, Melvin Brilliant, who read my first attempts to put words into memorable order and who, despite everything, encouraged me to write.

To my husband, Barr, and our son, Sam – love.

hope – a new constellation
waiting for us to map it,
waiting for us to name it – together
– Richard Blanco, *One Today*

"I listen to a few people I trust but not many."
– Flannery O'Connor

Secrets

E very day when I walk up to her with my pencil and a pad she orders the same thing: chef salad with Russian dressing and coffee. That's all we've said to each other. I nod, go get the stuff and bring it back to her. She smiles and our eyes meet. Her eyes are grey speckled: smooth stones lying next to the sea. Her skin is pale and her hair curls where it is not held back with barrettes. It reminds me of grass and wooden fences.

So far, she has never once brought a friend like most people – just a book for writing in. I've noticed too that she comes in at the same time. I begin to look forward to it. In this work I have time to notice these things. My job is monotonous and her visits are a relief.

As soon as she sits down, the air around her table forms a breathable shell shaped by her thoughts. She orders the salad, and when I bring it to her she eats quickly, bite after bite. But she's not rushed. She always stays for an hour. When I pour her first cup of coffee she slows down. She asks for a refill after carelessly lipping the cold ceramic rim; and sometimes she asks for a third and fourth cup while she writes.

And I'm certain she watches me. If I look over to see how she's doing, she's there looking back. So I smile.

She appreciates this and returns to her book. I resume placing orders, cleaning tables, wiping the counter top with a damp rag.

IT'S SUMMER NOW. Most of the women who come into the restaurant wear open V-neck blouses. The women who wear tight blazers are the executive types. They bring their briefcases to work. Then there are the men with the yellow pants, loafers and pink roll-up sleeve shirts – not my taste particularly.

My friend wears dungaree jumpsuits without sleeves – not my taste either – but her manners are. I like the way she sits at the table unconcerned that she is eating alone. I like the surefootedness of her voice. She speaks directly. Her eyes focus on me as if she knows who I am. Few people do.

Most people just comment on my hair. It's saffron gold and twists along the small of my back below my waist. I braid it for work. Even so, it gets in my way when I try to yank overstuffed bags of trash out of the barrels that contain them.

She is about the same height, same weight as me, but my arms are softer and her walk has more purpose. Anyway, I have this urge to follow her when she walks out the door each day and starts down the street. I consider it when I am scraping dirty plates or counting dimes and cents at the register.

Today she nods her head at me in the middle of her salad.

"Why are you working here?" she asks.

"Paying rent."

"You're miserable," she says. "I've seen you biting your lip. Your left hand is trembling."

"I'm recovering from suicidal tendencies," I answer, testing her response.

She smiles back in a way that is very pleased and approving; so I leave again and get on with my chores. I remain cryptic. I have never opened easily to people.

At the end of her lunch hour, I return with her check and again she smiles. I don't even look up to watch her walk out because I know she'll be back.

The following day I'm ready with her meal when she comes through the door.

"Why don't you meet me tomorrow after work?" she says. "We'll talk."

I peer inside her, pull back and scan the rest of her face.

"Fine," I say. "I'll wait for you here."

I go over to a booth and take orders from three good-looking men. They all have dark eyes, plump mouths.

"Who keeps you busy after work?" one of them asks.

"Three men," I joke. "More than I can keep track of."

Their eyes widen and their Adam's apples bounce up and down as they all laugh.

At four-thirty, I go into the bathroom, unbutton my uniform and slip on my dress. It's red. My skin is tanned. I brush out my hair with long, exacting strokes. Outside the women are looking at me. The men are honking. They should; I feel my eyes opening to the world. Now everybody wants to jump in.

I turn onto Commonwealth Avenue and walk toward the sun burning through leaf shadows. But in no time my perspiration feels like an irritation. I stop at an ice cream store and take a cooling break. Ice cream cones are soothing. Still, two miles later my dress is wrinkled and wet. The long strands of my hair have separated into gold streaks down my arm. Even the hallway of my building, which for a moment is cool and dark, grows hot. Nothing lasts. My apartment is roasting away. My cat is too tired to greet me.

I MIGHT HAVE known she wouldn't show. I waited forty minutes at work, drank two cups of coffee and left.

"I wasn't feeling well," she says the next day. "Don't be hurt."

I nod. I'm furious.

"I promise I'll come by tonight. You have a lovely face."

Only when I pick up her empty wooden bowl do I glance out the window and see her: an image through glass moving away. She disappears where the picture window ends. So I stare back into the bowl. There is one flat piece of onion skin at the bottom. It is what I know of her.

Late that afternoon, I bend over the ice cream cooler, taking care not to bump my elbow against the sticky metal sides.

"You through?" she says behind the counter.

"In twenty minutes."

"Good. I'll take a scoop then."

She sits at the table in the corner next to the wall.

"Do you have a lover?" she asks when I come out of the bathroom.

I think of him before answering.

"I did."

We walk out into the hot air. There's no wind along Massachusetts Avenue until we reach the bridge over the Charles where, grateful for the breeze, we stop midway to watch the sailboats. I smell her perfume of roses. The grainy stone of the bridge wall feels like a man's cheek. The sun and sky and air, boats with their white cloths flickering, flatten against the background of which we are the focus. I have a feeling of wanting her inside me; close. Instead, I stare down at the water.

"What are you thinking about?" she asks.

"Things," I say, turning to her.

"Like what? What's deadened you? Look at your face. You've got the eyes of a ninety-year-old."

I look back at the sailboats. The cars speeding behind us are waves bursting against rocks. Far out on the water, a boat moves as if sliding in mud, then slowly falls on its side. Its sails disappear beneath the surface. I watch the rescue boat leave from shore.

"I'm not dead," I say.

"Talk to me then," she whispers.

I feel the tips of my fingers scraping against the rock.

"You're asleep, under the surface," she continues.

"What surface?"

A car honks at us. The smell of the water is again lost in the traffic's exhaust.

"Let's move," I say. She seems to photograph my mind. I don't know if I like it.

"Listen," she persists. "Where have you been the last few years?"

"Places I can't rattle off standing on a bridge."

"Don't waste your time. You've wasted too much of it."

That's when she pivots and walks in a straight line toward Marlborough Street. I stand without moving, stunned, watching her walk away. Several yards off, she stops.

"Tomorrow!" she shouts.

I don't answer. I don't chase after her. There are still some daylight hours left and there's a man I like to watch in the Square. He juggles eggs and bowling pins, plates and hats.

The following day I don't predict what will occur between us, not even her salad.

"What can I get for you?"

"Come for dinner tonight."

"What about the bridge?"

"Tonight, we'll talk," she says. "No games."

I don't say anything.

"You're angry," she murmurs. "I can't help myself. I test people."

"I must have passed."

"Don't hold it against me," she says, touching my wrist. "You'll come?"

I nod.

She writes her name and address on a napkin, the "A" rising like a fir tree shadowing the smaller letters. The "Y" at the end of her name swirls like a smooth black whip.

Her apartment, a basement studio outside Kenmore Square, has two rooms: a kitchen and a combined living and bedroom. Overhead, the pipes hanging from the ceiling are painted white to blend with the walls. The wooden floor has been painted black. It is typical in most ways except for its lack of furniture. She touches my skirt.

"Drink something," she offers.

In the living room there is a table just inches off the floor. A wine bottle and two glasses have been placed there. The wine is pale and dry. It sucks my tongue when I sip it. I pour her glass and put it beside her plate.

"Three more minutes," she says coming back from the kitchen. She reaches for her glass.

"Did I tell you?" she begins. "I was living with a man for almost three months." She sweeps her glass through the air. "The furniture was his. I asked him to leave."

I look around for signs of him. There is an oversized shirt hanging on a nail next to the mattress in the corner.

"I'm glad we met," she says. "I don't like many people."

"You don't know me," I remind her.

Though the heat from the oven smells good, it is hard to breathe. Her windows are high up and small.

"I'll open the door," she says. "And we'll eat. I hope you like chicken."

"Is it safe here?"

"There was a voyeur," she calls from the kitchen. "In July. But my lover was here then. Now I dial the police."

We eat slowly. I glance at the bare walls and feel the moisture gathering on my shoulders. The room is darkening. Her face dissolves into the shadows. She isn't pretty. It is her eyes that draw me to her. We drink more wine.

"We met at a Laundromat last spring."

I listen carefully, nodding at each word.

"He moved in a month later. It was one of those things," she says. We both glance at the mattress on the floor. "You know, in bed most of the time or at the laundry washing the sheets. I got bored."

"I've never had that problem," I say. Her eyes are all I can see. "I dive in and don't get out."

"Your suicide. I can see that," she says, nodding. "Have some more wine. Where did you meet him?"

"I was working at another restaurant."

"And he was the owner?"

"That's right. He owned it. That's right." I wait for her to fill my glass. I feel her sponging knowledge from my brain. I don't want her to stop now.

"And so?"

"Every night he stood at the bar and talked to me when I came over to order drinks. He liked to chew on a straw when he talked. He was sly. I think it was a prop to show off his tongue."

She licks her teeth. "That was it?"

"No."

"Well?"

I swallow more wine.

"I hate cowboy clothes," I say. "They looked good on him though – dungarees and pointed boots. 'Aren't you lonely?' he'd ask."

"What'd you say?" Her voice demands. "You told him you masturbated thinking of him." She coughs, laughing to herself. I wait for her to come back to me. She empties her glass, thrusting her chin into the dark; then she crosses her legs and grins.

I try to ignore her behavior and continue. "On Saturday nights, a few of us stayed late drinking and talking. One night I stayed after everyone else had left. We were alone. I was drunk. He was chewing on his straw."

She flattens herself on the floor, folding her hands beneath her neck. "I understand completely. I do. I really do."

I push a chicken wing in a circle around my plate. I'm not sure what to say next; maybe nothing.

"Wait!" she says. She goes to the kitchen and brings back a long, slim candle. Its quiet flame moves like honey. We watch it for a while.

"Go on," she says. "Talk. I'm listening."

"He said he wanted to take me to a beach house he owned. He said he wanted to take me to a lot of places. We made love right there on the seat. He was married too. I saw him for two, three months."

"Listen," she says. "Why don't you stay? You can take a cool bath. I've got something you can sleep in. Tomorrow we can spend the day together. You're not in a rush, are you?"

During the night, the dark air filters through our bodies. We lie on opposite sides of the double bed. She faces the wall and sleeps. I face her back, keeping an arm's length distance between us. What is this weakening resistance I feel? Her legs jutting from her tee shirt are white and immobile and unappealing even. There are two moles on the inner crease of her knee. Her shirt is the same color as her thighs.

I listen. Sounds from the street whisper to me through the windows as if to explain. But the windows are like radio speakers turned down too low. I strain and cannot decipher what I hear. I shift onto my back. At odd intervals, water from the pipes rushes through the plumbing above and into the wall to somewhere beyond. Maybe I have said too much. I turn on my hip and place my palms under my eyes, not wanting morning to come. Time passes. I watch her body slowly change with the light.

She makes coffee in the morning. I act as though I have done this before. It's not as if anything has happened, I remind myself. Relax. Sit on the floor. Lean back against the cool refrigerator.

Her old lover's shirt hangs over my knees. She stands at the sink comically exposed in her underwear, her excess bosom vibrating as she sponges the dirty plates. She's proud of her large breasts, a pride I've never cared about; mine are small.

"Want me to do that?" I ask. She is scrubbing the sink, jerking her elbow in the air with each stroke.

"I need to get out of here," she says, dropping the sponge.

The haze coming through the window casts shadows that blur on the floor, a light that looks cold; yet the hairs on my skin are flattened by a sticky, warm glaze.

"You never said why it ended," she adds, wiping her forehead. "You never did."

"It's not important."

She nods and says nothing. Perhaps she is judging me, or bored, or both.

"It's important," she says. "Come on. What's the secret?"

"There was another woman. I saw them in a car in the parking lot, okay?"

"I'm not surprised," she answers, leaving the room.

She dresses, wearing the dungaree skirt she often wears to work and a green bikini top, its green hues seeping into her eyes. I get dressed too and wait for more; I can feel it.

"What's your father like?" she practically shouts.

"Problematic. Why?"

"You fell in love with your father."

"I don't know." I slide back down against the wall to the floor. "What are you saying?"

"He didn't take you seriously. Did he?" She stands over me. "Did he?"

I look up at the shadow in her face. "Who?"

"I bet you felt used. You felt used, didn't you? You wanted to marry him."

She stares at me. I turn away. The wooden planks on the floor fly out in a pattern that reminds me of the gym my mother used to go to when I was a child.

"Hey, don't turn your head. Look at me. He took the soul out of you. I can see it. You have no idea who you – "

"You're no different," I murmur, squeezing my eyelids to make her stop.

She stoops in front of me. "I'm so sorry," she whispers.

We look at each other. For a moment, I let her finger my braid; then I get up and walk back to the kitchen for some water. She follows me.

"Are you going to forgive me?"

I wait for the water to cool down and fill the glass that has been left in the sink.

"You're miserable, but you don't want to get out of it," she says. "Don't you see? I care. That's why I'm telling you."

"We need to get out of here," I say.

She looks at me and touches my shoulder, relieved. She's happy that I have asserted myself. Her smile is terrible and sweet. I go outside and wait by the curb while she double-locks her door. Half the day has passed.

"HERE. YOU TAKE this," she says, handing me a chocolate cone. She orders strawberry. We adjust our napkins and walk to the river, toward the clouds overhanging it. She points to the shapes in the sky. "Round bottoms waiting to be fucked," she says.

At the riverbank, we find a tree to sit under. I watch a group of scullers approach. They skim the water the way birds migrate north in the sky, forming a V. Rows of men thrust backward and forward. I feel their movement in my head.

Slowly she too, once again, pulls and pushes, more carefully this time. What about my mother, she asks. Do I have any sisters? Did I do well in school?

"My mother is fine," I answer. "I have one older sister. I don't have any brothers. I did well in school. Why so many questions?" I ask.

"No more. Tell me one dream, a good one and I won't ask any more." She laughs, childlike. "Or a fantasy, it doesn't matter which." Her eyes spin and she flops back on the grass.

"I've always wanted to travel." I say this with a question in my voice, sitting with my back as straight as I can manage.

"Everyone travels," she says. "What's stopping you?" She looks at the horizon. "Never mind. We'll talk about that the next time. I forgot. I've got to get home. I told this person I would meet him tonight. It's late. I didn't realize how late; look at the sky. I should have known."

She stands up and holds out her hand. "All right? You don't mind? We're friends?"

I take her hand but I know as she grips my palm it is another insane game.

"You've got that tense look on your face," she says. "Let go of my hand. Let go. Goodbye."

She starts to skip away toward the crowded square. This time I want to chase after her, walk her home, make plans for another day. But she quickens her pace, running now, as if she has heard my feelings. So I stay seated, hugging my knees. She grows smaller, blurred, and when she reaches the opposite end of the field, I lose sight of her in a shimmer of human beings.

Monday, the following day, she doesn't come in. On Tuesday, when I get home from work, I call her. Her line rings and rings all night. Wednesday, it's the same. Twice, I stop at the graphics shop where she works and leave a note. Each day, according to the receptionist, she isn't there. Finally, Thursday, determined to gain some control, I leave early to catch her.

At the customer service window a man directs me to a door that leads to the basement. The stairs are dusty and as I walk around the bend in the steps, I see her on a stool next to a counter littered with strips of film.

"I've been looking for you," I call out.

She holds one of the strips to the light. She doesn't look at me.

"So I hear. Here I am," she replies. Her head turns slowly and her eyes, once they are focused, are flat as photographs.

"Why haven't you come to see me?" I ask. My voice is a frayed rope, weak and unsafe.

"We're not lovers, you know. I've been busy. What do you want? Well?"

I turn back into the shadow of the staircase and retrace my steps.

FOR WEEKS AFTER I drift through the lunch hours. My flesh, sucked of its blood, is dry as paper. I imagine if these two glasses of water, which I am balancing on my tray, were to spill against me, my skin would disappear. I've learned not to expect her and she never comes.

I think I will feel unburdened when she has left this town, moved to Minnesota to begin a new job. Three days ago when I passed her on the street, she said we would have to get together before she leaves. She asked how I was. In that October light, I glimpsed a sketch of something I knew and continued on.

Having arrived at the booth with the couple in it, I carefully set their glasses to the right of their plates. They turn and smile at me. I blink, raising the pencil, which I have sharpened, to my lips and wait for their order. I hear secret voices in my head: men and women wanting from me; me wanting from them. I nod like the waitress that I am, obliging their requests. Why don't you do this or that? Fulfill so we can love.

I look up at the clock. "It'll only take a few minutes. That's it," I say to the couple who want sandwiches. I start for the grill. This is temporary. All of this is. I stop to lift a chair out of the aisle and accelerate, clearing the way for myself in this crowd.

Papier-mâché

I f they try to intimidate you, Leah thought, picture them naked. She stared at Professor Steiler's breasts. The professor turned and walked to the opposite end of the table to where Elaine Tyson sat. Elaine was the pathologically shy one in the class.

"Art should excite the emotions," Steiler explained. "Particularly emotions of fear. Ms. Tyson would you comment – "

"Why is that?" Leah said, interrupting.

"Fear is the source of the sublime." The older woman crossed the room and stood by Jim Cancela. "Mr. Cancela?" What is your idea of the sublime?"

"Not this place," Leah muttered.

Jim Cancela puckered his lips. He was Steiler's favorite, the blameless class pet. Naturally, Leah disliked him.

"What about the apples?" Leah called out. "The way they make you want to curl your fingers around them? Feel them." She thrust her hand toward the center of the conference table.

Steiler walked over to the window and looked out. The other eleven students, except Leah, concentrated on their fingernails. Even Michael Ford, who typically sat next to Leah, and in addition felt it his duty to affirm anything that Leah said during class, usually by nodding or saying, "right," remained mum.

"Feeling, Ms. Fineburg," Steiler said to the window-pane, "is an obscure word. Space and color are specific elements that help us define it." She turned back and faced the class. Leah noticed that the rouge on Steiler's face did not blend with the jawbone and that the shade of lipstick made the woman's skin look tired and green.

"Let's return to our painting here," Steiler said.

At the front of the room a poster mounted on a tri-pod showed a portrait of a young woman reading. Next to her, a bowl of apples shone in a halo of light from a window behind the young woman's head. Leah imag-ined changing places with the woman in the painting, sitting in the scarlet oversized chair, the varnish on the wooden table gleaming beside her. It was a wonderful place to get away from it all until the picture fell from the tripod and slid to the floor. Naturally, Jim Cancela, a dark-skinned, quiet boy, was the one to pick it up. Leah watched him disappear under the table. Steiler smiled and thanked him. Michael elbowed Leah.

After class, Leah bolted down the stairs and started for home, a one bedroom in Allston, but changed her mind and walked instead to the nicer section of Coolidge Corner in Brookline. It was aberrantly hot for April. Four o'clock in the afternoon and she was sweating from the heat. It was unnatural for New England unless one considered that Boston natives, including Leah, thrived on the city's erratic weather patterns. It was a cultural sickness, a geographical neurosis she decided as she passed a group of elderly women on a bench in front of the bus stop, their sweat-ers pushed up to their elbows. She stopped to look at a pinstriped suit in a window display, then went into the store to try it on. She wore pants every day of her college life.

The two-piece outfit didn't fit: too snug at the shoulders, too ungainly at the hips. So, I'm a fool, she said to herself in the dressing room mirror, tugging at the material. Dress-you-down-rooms she called them. The carpet was always the same grey, trapping fallen straight pins, which stung her feet. The rooms lacked for hooks, a place to hang unwanted clothes. She put her uniform back on, army pants and tee shirt, and left.

Everyone was out: mothers with babies, college students, *bizarro* types. Up ahead, a woman in a white fur hooded jacket, pink tights and ballet shoes lunged forward. Leah walked faster for a closer look while others coming in the opposite direction slowed down as they passed the displaced ballerina. The dancer veered into the street, and several cars honked as she tiptoed across during a green light. Leah worried suddenly that the ballerina would catch an ungainly leg on a car fender and end up in a sponge of blood and fur. But nothing happened. The ballerina made it across and miraculously disappeared into a cross-town bus waiting at the corner stop. People like that had a way of avoiding the obvious dangers in life; but not the harm of tyrannical parents, rapes, incest, bigotry, fear, deceit.

SHE PATTED HER damp forehead with the bottom of her shirt and walked in to her first floor apartment. Not wanting to waste her stipend on rent, she had converted the former living room into a second bedroom and asked Tilly, also a scholarship student, to share the expense.

"I got a ninety-eight in biology today," Tilly announced from the kitchen. Tilly gained weight like a man – in the midriff and under her chin. She could control her grades but not her eating habits. Leah didn't have weight issues but had peculiar tastes. She liked mixing bran cereal into a quart of chocolate ice cream. She could live on that for days.

"Fascinating. I'll be in the shower. Don't get me out if anyone calls."

"Your mother?" Tilly called back.

Leah closed the bathroom door and didn't respond. Tilly knew damn well she'd rather not talk to her mother.

THE FOLLOWING WEEK in class, several students failed to show up due to heavy rain, which made the dark room gloomy and desolate.

"I have your papers," Steiler announced. The professor sat at the head of the table and folded her hands. "Overall, you didn't do too badly. I've seen worse. I always enjoy getting to know you. Certainly, I learn a great deal about you from the initial assignment." Steiler lifted herself out of her chair and handed back the papers.

Leah took hers and was aghast at the abundant mass of pen marks that culminated in a mediocre grade at the bottom of the page. She couldn't remember ever getting a C and felt nauseous. Listening to Steiler talk about good writing made her feel worse. Jim Cancela, at Steiler's request, read a passage from his paper. Michael tried to get Leah to tell him what she got but she refused.

"Let's continue with our presentations," Steiler said. "Why don't you begin, Ms. Tyson?"

The others waited for Elaine, who struggled miserably to talk.

"Rough Sea," Elaine whispered.

"Who? Please speak up," Steiler said.

The woman's a sadist, Leah thought.

"I've chosen Rough Sea by Monet." Elaine coughed. "Rough Sea, as you can see," she said, raising the color-plated book for the class. "Uh, you will notice that," she turned to look at the page; "You will notice. I noticed that the two men looked out of proportion sort of like a Japanese print."

"We're not discussing Japanese art," Steiler said.

"She's making a connection," Leah said.

"Fabrication," Steiler replied. "Learn the difference. Continue please, Ms. Tyson."

"Well, you see," Elaine said. "I was visualizing the sea as a cloud on top of a canyon even though the boats show we are really viewing the tide. But for the moment I imagined being on top of the canyon looking down at the clouds and also that the cliffs on the upper left side – "

"Ms. Tyson, focus on the color and form that already exist in the painting rather than conjuring up some imagined object."

"Why separate them?" Leah asked. "Imagination has everything to do with forms that already exist."

"You're a show," Michael whispered beside her. Leah ignored him. Steiler pressed her fingers in prayer formation and raised her chin.

"It's not whether we are separating these things, Ms. Fineburg. The question is whether we are able to perceive the particular elements which made up this whole."

Leah nodded and wondered if Steiler used unscented soap. She hoped so because the famous professor was wearing the same skirt again. Obviously the woman imagined herself differently than how she appeared. Leah decided not to say anything for the remainder of the class. But afterward, she followed Steiler to her office one floor below.

"I knew you would be upset with the grade," Steiler said sitting down at her desk. "The problem, Ms. Fineburg, is your lack of order. Clear writing reflects clear thinking."

Leah scowled and leaned against the doorframe. Sure thing, Leah thought. She scanned the walls. They were covered with photographs of famous artists' faces, their names signed in pen near the frame. Art books filled every bookshelf. Stacks of books rose like chimneys at each corner of the floor. Steiler hunkered over the old wooden desktop. The desk had enough space on it for a phone, an empty cookie wrapper beside the phone, more books, and a tiny-framed picture of a young man.

"I normally do better than this, much better," Leah said. "I've been away. My brother died." She hadn't meant to say this but there it was. Her brother committed suicide.

"I'm sorry to hear that," Steiler said. "But your problems are not unlike most of the students' work I see presently. I can recommend two books to assist you."

"As I said, this isn't typical of me. Who's that?" She pointed to the picture on the desk.

"My son. Here you are." Steiler held out the paper with the names but Leah ignored the gesture.

"What does your son do?"

"He doesn't know. He can't commit himself to anything."

Leah nodded sagely, detecting a weak spot in the impenetrable professor.

"Committing isn't everything," Leah said. "Do you have any other children?"

"No. Now, is there anything else you'd like to discuss?"

"No." Leah left without taking the sheet of paper.

She went across the street to the college coffee shop and ordered sliced apples and milk. She had an hour to kill before therapy. Dr. May McNulty specialized in alternative methods of psychoanalysis – Gestalt, meditation – but more importantly, Leah liked her the first time they met. The college support center had given Leah the referral when she returned to school after Aaron's funeral and the weeklong period of mourning, the previous spring.

Dr. May, as Leah liked to call her, was direct but gentle and didn't insist that Leah go through the four stages of grief like her mother did. She looked like a former gymnast: petite and energetic, exacting in her physical movements.

A waiter on roller skates with green hair and a red silk tie took Leah's order. He was one of the reasons she came to this restaurant. He didn't appear to care what people thought of him. The waiter rolled back and placed the bowl of apples in front of her. They were arranged in the shape of a lotus flower. She was sure there was something hidden in Steiler, something soft and weak. Everyone had that. She would make Steiler listen to her. She inspected one of the apple slices, then bit it in half.

"GET COMFORTABLE," DR. May said from across the heavily furnished, carpeted room. "We're going to try some directed visualization today." The therapist's office was in a renovated attic of Brookline's mini-estate area, not far from President Kennedy's childhood home. Once a week, Leah passed the historic home but had yet to go inside it. She had enough death to think about.

She stretched out on the couch and pushed her shoes off, fitting between the two couch arms. As she followed Dr. May's instructions to close her eyes, Steiler's face emerged in the darkness like a solid object in a dark pool. The woman had become an obsession. Dr. May encouraged her to let every image come through and in no time she saw Elaine Tyson's greasy hair and her mother's oversized, wasted eyes, then a sketch of her brother, Aaron, beneath a white cotton blanket. Aaron had an angular face and a bicyclist's body, taut as rope. The cotton blanket changed to a rippling waterfall. Leah nestled deeper into the sofa as Dr. May asked her to talk about what she saw.

"A waterfall."

She leaned over a boulder to feel the water gushing over a pile of smaller rocks. Soft car noises from the residential street in Brookline mingled with the water sound. A bicycle bell rang and a small truck shifted gears. Flowers grew out of the rocky mountainside. She went over and picked one; then she heard the bicycle bell again.

"What do you see now?" Dr. May asked.

The waterfall drifted away and Leah saw the green lawn of her childhood home, oak trees, the chain link fence that separated their yard from the neighboring woods, a blue sky. She saw Aaron and a middle-aged woman holding a kite.

"This lady, Mrs. Devonshire, stayed with us once for a week. My parents were away, before their divorce. Mrs.

Devonshire taught Aaron how to make a kite. I made a tree. We used papier-mâché." She remembered the sticky white paste on her hands. "I planted my tree in the back-yard. It lasted four days before the rain got it. But we still have Aaron's kite."

She opened her eyes. "I don't know," Leah said, struggling to get up. She felt dizzy. Why hold on to things that are gone? She hated the overhead light and covered her face. Was she supposed to sit there and cry?

"You'll be all right," Dr. May said, walking over and sitting next to Leah on the couch.

Leah talked into her hands. "Please don't touch me. And don't tell me I'll be okay. I hate that. It's so typical."

WHEN SHE GOT home, Tilly handed Leah the phone. "Your mother."

"I just walked in," Leah said to the receiver.

"Jewel, honey."

"Don't call me Jewel, Mother."

"Don't be mean. I'm your mother and I'm alone here."

Leah looked at an old wire running along the mold-ing on the wall.

"Don't you forget that," her mother continued.

"How could I? You won't let me."

The phone disconnected. Leah waited for a dial tone and called her mother back.

'Mother, please. Maybe you should talk to a therapist. That's what I'm doing."

Her mother remained silent. What now, Leah thought.

"A therapist is not my family," her mother said. The phone disconnected again.

• • •

As LEAH LAY in bed that night the full moon whitened her room. Her body quivered and she saw the furniture vibrate in the light as if it were painted in air. The legs of the bureau mixed with the hairs in the rug. The red apples in the postcard she had pinned to the corner of her dresser mirror bobbed on the mercuric surface. She closed her eyes. A flash of white fur spun through her mind. A tree appeared and Leah saw herself standing beneath it, looking up at the stars. The ballerina, her pink legs floating behind like fish whiskers, hovered over Leah and the tree. Leah reached up to touch the dancer's shoe but the shoe became formless and trickled away in Leah's sleep.

The next day in class, Michael nudged her a few times and twisted his head in a questioning posture but Leah disappointed him again. Poor Michael couldn't adjust to the fact that she didn't want to talk anymore: not to him, anyone or anything. Period. Words had not helped her communicate. What did he expect? Besides, Steiler's zipper had been safety-pinned together. This was far more compelling to Leah.

Steiler must have had a bad morning. Her blouse was sweat stained. The scarf around her neck looked like it had been hanging on a door knob in a dead person's closet. While Steiler talked about colors and space, raising her arm to illustrate something, showing that stain again, Leah imagined the forty-ish old woman struggling to get dressed in the bedroom of an old brownstone apartment in front of a mirror that was also cracked and stained. Now Steiler was saying something about Cezanne and that whole impressionist crowd, quoting Pissaro, Cassatt, and the ballet man, Degas – the professor's voice tracing halos around Leah's head. She found it easy to condense Steiler's words into abstract sensations so that they no longer had meaning, only sound. When class ended, Leah passed her second paper to the front, along with the others, and headed home. She took care with this paper, rechecking and editing her analysis of an early Manet painting to avoid making the mistakes of the first assignment.

STEILER AVERTED HER eyes when she handed Leah the second graded paper. *You've been reading, as far as I can judge,* the professor scrawled, *some critics on the Masters. I'll have to see what you've used before I can judge how much of this is yours. Resubmit with Xeroxes of materials consulted.* There was no grade.

"You've accused me of plagiarism," Leah said, standing inside the door frame of Steiler's office.

"My instincts are usually right," Steiler said. She leaned back in her chair, her cheekbones protruding like knife handles. "Perhaps you would like to tell me what papers you've used?"

"You specifically asked that we not use outside sources, isn't that right? Which means you are calling me a liar."

Steiler's head twitched.

"Perhaps I'm mistaken. Nonetheless, I'd have to see some of your previous essays to determine that. Compared to your first paper, this one clearly surpasses what you seem capable of."

"I'll get those papers to you." Leah glanced over at the portraits on the wall. Steiler herself looked like an oversized plaster bust. She's out of her mind. Out of this world.

Leah ran down two flights of stairs into the wind outside. Overhead the sky sucked up the last shadows on the street. She could smell rain but she headed down to the Copley Square, the opposite direction from home, and took an elevator forty-six stories into the clouds.

From the John Hancock building, she looked out over the balcony to the rooftops, the highways twisting through fields surrounding the city. The sky had darkened, clumping like soiled cotton. She had a sudden impulse to jump free and grabbed hold of the railing to check herself. Aaron had slid a needle into his vein. That was the end of it. Who was he? She remembered how he had screamed at her once for misplacing his pen. She had thought all older brothers did that. Then he had nearly twisted her elbow off despite the fact that he'd had a whole drawer full of replacements. Her brother had been a heroin addict. She followed the railing around to the other side of the building and leaned against it.

The moment between the balcony and the pavement would be the most difficult. All those tiny human beings moving senselessly below, what would they do if she flung herself, arms and legs splayed like Aaron's kite, fluttered through the air for a few moments of grace before breaking into the impenetrable? It might take her to the purest sense of herself: no place – no up or down. She walked back inside and went home.

She knelt on her bedroom rug and rifled through old term papers. That woman was not going to get away with this. A's and B's; words on the pages that said *insightful, original, penetrating* spread in a circle around her. Tilly wasn't home yet. The rain had started and it was dark but Leah did not want to turn on the light.

"So you're home," her mother said after Leah picked up the phone.

"I'm home."

"What's wrong? I can hear something in your voice."

"Nothing. I'm studying."

"I'm not going to fight with you dear. Aaron's anniversary is in three weeks. I want you home for that. I want you home and I'm not going to worry about it. You make promises and you break them. Do you ever think of your mother?"

"Never. Almost every day," Leah said, looking down the end of her dark hall. Her mother lived in Portland, Maine, a two-hour bus ride she didn't want to take. She left the papers on the floor and lay down on the bed. The woman in a fur-lined world held out her hand. Leah took hold of it in her sleep.

At her subsequent therapy session, the thought of the waterfall, which Dr. May asserted was Leah's inner place of solace and rest, embarrassed and annoyed her. Seeing the sofa reminded her of all that. She crossed the room and sat in a chair next to the door. Dr. May looked calm. That annoyed her too.

"Leah?" Dr. May said.

Leah picked up a magazine about dogs and flipped the pages until she found something that interested her: *A Couple's Nightmare.*

"What's going on with you right now?"

"Nothing." Exactly that, Leah thought and began reading … *An elderly couple from Maryland was attacked while staying at the Eagle Lake Motel. Inadequate safety measures —*

"Leah?

... made it easy for intruders to enter the room where the Bancrofts were sleeping. They had not used the locks on their door and guests who heard the commotion did nothing for fear the intruders —

"Leah, did something happen this week?"

Mr. Bancroft was beaten with a metal rod sustaining multiple injuries —

"Leah, I'm not going to judge you if you want to tell me."

Leah looked up. Dr. May's hair was pinned in a tiny knot on top of her head, like a dancer's.

OVER THE WEEKEND, Leah sat in front of the television and went to a German subtitled movie with Tilly at the Coolidge independent film theater. The last scene showed a woman in bed, a vial of pills scattered on the sheets: symbol of a ruined life.

"Is that the only option?" Tilly wanted to know as they walked home.

"I can't talk about it," Leah said. It was dusk and car lights popped out of the dim air like fireflies.

Tilly nodded and hurried to keep up with Leah.

"You know Steiler's whole problem?" Leah began. "She's divorced. The secretary told me."

"That's not your problem," Tilly said.

"Yes, it is," Leah said, halting on the sidewalk for emphasis. Sometimes Tilly's penchant for cheap advice infuriated her. "If you don't mind, I think I'd like to walk the rest of the way home alone."

She crossed the street and cut through a ballpark, following a white line that formed one side of the baseball field. Steiler's bitter way was more than a problem. It was an oppression. Leah slowed down under the streetlights.

A stray cat emerged from a hedge and she called to it but it was wary and slunk back under the shrub. When she got home Tilly was hidden away in the bedroom. They had gotten into spats like this many times.

The following day, Leah sat in class with her stack of papers, hands folded in her lap. Michael pulled up a chair but said nothing. One by one the others took their places and waited.

It surprised Leah how short Steiler was, petite really with bony shoulders and small hands. Petite except for those wide, inner tube hips she hid beneath the conference table once Steiler sat down.

"I'd like each of you to choose one of the three topics written on this sheet," Steiler said, passing the sheet around. "A five minute talk will suffice."

Reading the list – influences, topography, subject – Leah wondered if Steiler had been shafted by her husband as her mother had been.

"Ms. Tyson, let's begin," Steiler said, returning to the seat at the head of the table.

Leah was sure Steiler picked on Tyson for the pure joy of it.

Elaine twirled a pen in her hand and pushed the bangs from her eyes. Three students opened their notebooks and started doodling.

"There is always the problem of determining influences."

"True," Steiler said.

True, Leah mimicked.

"Yes ... so, um ... "

Moving along, Leah thought. Her temples itched from Elaine's endless hesitations.

"There's the influence of the teacher over the artist, the way a parent influences a child."

The parent will do it to you every time, Leah agreed. "The critic to the work of art."

"Naturally," Steiler nodded, going in for the kill. "But let's start with one. We're not asking you to address every option, Ms. Tyson."

We? Leah thought, digging her pen into a groove in the table until the plastic cap snapped under the pressure. Several people looked at her.

She could not listen any longer and stared at the pile of papers to prove her teacher wrong. What had Aaron been thinking? The nurses had opened the curtains that last day so that the sunlight fell on his face but no light penetrated him. He was gone. Steiler called on another student until a half a dozen students had given impromptu speeches.

"Leah!" Steiler said. "You may begin."

Leah focused on two aluminum eyes, the woman's narrow face, the brown sweater and roundish body quivering, the tiny hands curling into themselves.

"I would like to discuss the critic's relationship to art," Leah began.

"What specifically?" Steiler asked.

"If the critic focuses on abstract ideas as a way of responding emotionally to the work, she ends up confusing concepts with emotion. Intellectual constructs become a way of feeling. Theories, not emotions, form a grid through which the critic perceives or misperceives the art. This is a danger," Leah continued, seeing her words reflecting across her brain. "For it is another way the critic convinces herself that she is being objective or right. The intellect," she said, clicking the t's, "just like everything else human, rearranges ideas in the way it prefers and that, after all, is just another way of being subjective. Take color, for example – "

"Whose idea might that be?" Steiler asked.

Leah heard footsteps out in the hall. Chairs scraped against the floor. The period had ended. Several people stood up to leave.

"Mine," she said. "I have my own ideas."

Steiler nodded and gathered her things.

"Excuse me," Leah said. "But I've brought my papers." She looked at Michael, who was slowly getting out of his seat, then back at Steiler who had embraced her books and was starting for the door.

"I'd like you to look at these papers," Leah said.

Michael buttoned his coat and finally left. The room was empty now.

"Impossible, I have an out of town lecture. I won't be back until after the weekend."

"I'm not waiting a week. If you'd rather, I'll file a complaint with the Dean."

Steiler shifted her stance. "I can't stop you from doing that."

"Yes, you could. It won't take long to look at these." She held the papers and shook them.

"Next week would be better for me."

"What's the matter with you? Look at yourself," Leah said, raising her voice. "Your clothes. Your loneliness – "

"That's enough."

"No. It isn't. You called me a liar."

Steiler walked over to the door and pulled it shut.

"I'm going to ask you to remove yourself from my seminar. This is impossible."

"I am simply asking you to read these papers. And no. You won't do it! You insult me!" Leah cried out. "Your husband left you and I can see why. Didn't he?" She stood in the room wavering in the clammy air. The windows lining the wall resembled cut-out pieces of cardboard. What would it take to make her pay attention? Leah wondered.

Steiler looked at her and reached for the papers in her hand.

"Sit down, Leah."

They sat. Steiler rummaged through her briefcase for reading glasses and began comparing essays. Leah stared at nothing, at the wall, at Aaron's peaceful, breathless face until finally Steiler looked up at her.

"You don't like me," Leah said, "But it would be difficult to change courses at this point."

"You say unpleasant things, even if I were mistaken."

The professor handed Leah the newly graded essay; not her best grade, but certainly not her worst.

Leah nodded. She looked at Steiler's face. The mouth stripped of lipstick was pale and the eyes behind the near-sighted glasses hinted at a softer, more delicate light. Seeing that, Leah wanted to say she knew what it was like to lose somebody. They had that in common didn't they? Instead she nodded again and spared them both by walking out.

Boarders

J ennifer was gaunt and rangy looking when she
dropped out of a tiny women's college in Vermont
to figure out what she wanted from life and to be with
Kevin in Boston. Things with Kevin were cresting haz-
ardously and she couldn't see beyond the narrow stall of
four more months sharing a room in a dorm filled with
dozens of lonely, single women.

Only one semester into it, her action surprised everyone including herself – a break from the safety zone – a
swan dive into deeper space, her darker core. But going
back home to her parents' in Brighton, a dense, mixed
housing section of Boston, had been a mistake. Her
father prodded incessantly. "Get a job like everyone else."
The second week home, she started waitressing at a local
steak house. Still, he kept after her. *Did she think she had
special privileges? Did she think she was going to get a free
ride?* There was no relief until she saw Mr. Ledger's room
for rent in the local paper.

Just blocks away, Ledger's Victorian had everything she
needed. A brass bed, two wall sconces adorned with crystal bracelets, and wallpaper with large pink flowers, pink
as her lipstick except where the radiator had turned the

flowers brown – as if the room had been waiting for her. Mr. Ledger himself seemed nice enough. He was an elderly man, skinny and tall, who kept his pants hiked up with a belt.

Now the room was hers. No badgering father. Just silence. She touched the furnishings to be sure, pulling open the wide, curved bureau drawers, checking the hot-plate atop the half refrigerator. Her books she piled on the floor. She would organize the rest of her things later, clothes and toiletries mashed into one frayed orange suit-case lined with silken material that paled decades ago, the kind of luggage that shut with a gold-plated latch. She went to the window beside the bed and watched a branch shake in the January chill before going down to get something to eat in town.

On the way downstairs she looked for signs of the other two boarders, two older men who, according to Ledger, lived down the hall from her. But the house appeared empty, except for Mr. Ledger who sat in a wing chair by the living room window, reading.

"Where did you say you were working?" Mr. Ledger called to her.

"The Steak House, not far from here."

"You wish to pursue a career as a waitress?"

"No, no," she said, smiling. "Pretty room," she said, in a friendly attempt to divert him from her personal life. Reflection was not on her agenda right now. The room had large bay windows, a grand piano and a space heater that had been carefully positioned near his chair.

"Yes, the light is good for reading. But I don't want anyone sitting there," he said, pointing. "That was my wife's sewing room."

She turned to the room on the opposite side of the downstairs hall. Two chairs and a divan had been strung up with kite string. "Of course not," she said. She tossed her overgrown blond bangs out of her eyes and started for the door but he hadn't finished.

"Did you study Latin in school?" he asked. "I used to teach Latin at the high school."

"I did for two years. *Laudo, laudas*," she began. "*Laudat, laudatis*."

"*Laudamus*," he corrected her.

"*Laudamus*," she laughed, hoping he would let her go now.

"One more thing," he said. "I don't allow men upstairs in your room."

"What about downstairs?"

"In the hallway is fine," he said, and went back to reading.

She hadn't expected this but said nothing. She walked the short distance to town and bought bread and cheese and milk.

Upon her return an hour later, she passed the empty wing chair, the bathroom and the phone table at the top of the stairs. Then she headed toward the opposite end of the hall to her room. Still, no sign of the two boarders. She closed her door.

From her toiletry bag she uncapped a vial of sleeping pills leftover from her ailing grandfather before he died of heart failure. She took one and spilled the rest into the night table drawer by the bed. Next she leafed through a biology text, memorizing organs – her latest interest. She took another pill after reading about adrenal glands and soon a pleasant, woozy feeling of trees swayed in her head. Kevin came to mind but she decided not to call him. He had been too preoccupied lately, bent over the piano like a man tending to his dying lover. The conservatory took up the rest of his time. She got into bed and let the pills massage her to sleep.

All week she reported to the restaurant. She went to Kevin's over the weekend. She liked him best naked, murmuring *pianissimo* into her neck – his word of course. But more and more she lay alone on his bed listening as his hands fluttered across the baby grand his rich aunt had given him. He played for hours. After a year of seeing him in high school, she expected more from him since she had returned to live in the same city. "Remember me?" she called to him.

He came into the bedroom and she shifted on the mattress to make room for him. His bed was narrow and old but his hazel eyes drew her to him like invisible strings.

"I've got to practice, you know that," he said.

"I know. You don't have to say it." He told her this at least once a day and this, too, began to sound like an admonition, another person urging her to find something better to do than what she had chosen for herself. She pulled on his shirt and they kissed. He rolled over her and soon they had shed what was in the way of their skin, rocking against the headboard; the wind in her head clearing out doubting thoughts. They rolled apart and Kevin lit a cigarette. They lay side by side, smoking.

"Kev! Buddy boy! Open up!"

Jay and Alan, Kevin's friends from school, beat on the front door in rhythmic thumps. They had come to take them to Michele's party. Michele played the flute and practiced duets with Kevin. She was a small woman, deceptively demure and one of the reasons Jennifer felt compelled to return to Boston. Michele had a talent for creating reasons to be with Kevin, usually to practice.

She had unearthed more piano flute duets in the last month than Jennifer believed existed. Now this party to lure Kevin over again.

"I'll get the door," she said. She rose from the bed and put on his terrycloth robe, the one he used after showers. It smelled of cigarettes and deodorant.

She walked down a short hall to the front door. He lived on the second floor of an apartment building near Symphony Hall. The neighborhood was a musician's nesting ground. Jazz guitarists from nearby Berklee music school paced the sidewalks late at night like adrenaline-loaded police in search of roving gigs. Classical pianists, like Kevin, took over the day shift clocking in six, ten hours of practice in order to play the notes exactly right.

"We were sleeping," she said nudging open the door. Dank air swept across her bare knees and toes. "God, it's cold," she said.

"You're looking good, Jen," Alan said, smiling at her.

"Looking madly," she said, smiling back provocatively. She was attracted to Alan. He had an athletic air about him and treated her as if she were the end zone and he were carrying the winning ball.

"Beer's in the kitchen," Kevin said, stepping out fully clothed.

She sauntered back to the bedroom, aroused by Alan's arrival, and shimmied into her pantyhose, black skirt, black bra, black button down sweater. She liked Alan's carelessness, his weathered complexion. Kevin avoided the outdoors. Only after sex or a concert did his face, angular, white as sheet music, flush with renewed blood.

"I'll have one too," she said, entering the small kitchen where the threesome stood in a small circle guzzling. Alan opened the refrigerator and handed her one.

"Especially for you," he said. He took another for himself.

"Especially thank you." She turned sideways to give him a fuller silhouette, her breasts still tingling from Kevin's mouth. When she first met Alan she guessed that he played drums, but she was wrong. He told her that the Clarinet had its own power and could snake its way across any jungle of sounds.

She shifted toward Kevin again but he started for the front door. Jay, the most docile of the group followed.

"Are we in a rush?" she called to Kevin.

But he didn't answer her. By the time she and Alan reached the street downstairs, Kevin had already seized the front seat of Jay's car: a bronze Jetta with two shoe-size dents on the driver's side. She gave Kevin an inquisitive look but he continued to ignore her as she slipped behind him to the back seat, next to Alan.

With everyone in the car, Jay started the motor. "Party time," he said, turning out of the parking space.

"Have another sip of beer. Relax," Alan told her. He handed her his can.

She took it, licking the icy drops from the aluminum sides and drank thirstily. Outside, the sky amassed into a brown, blood-colored night. The trees bare and isolated from each other were silent as the back of Kevin's head.

She took another sip then drank ravenously, tapping the last tinny drops onto her lips, making sure all was gone. Jay turned on the radio and for a short while they all listened to the evening news: the governor wanted to raise taxes. Picketers against same sex marriage had caused a traffic hold-up outside the State house. A famous actress had died.

"Same old shit," Alan said.

Jay put his demo CD into the player. His blues-driven guitar backed by years of classical training, including flamenco, came through the strings with clarity and warmth. The effect settled the edginess mounting in the car as they drove west down Commonwealth Ave. to Kenmore Square past burger joints and curbsides garnished with litter. Alan pointed to a billboard looming over the Square: a photo of a naked woman riding bareback on a white horse.

"My kind of girl," Alan said. He flicked his tongue and grinned.

"Funny, I had a different impression," Kevin said.

"Kevin," she said, touching his arm. "He's joking."

"I don't think so." He leaned away from her and turned up Jay's demo.

It was a pattern between Kevin and her. The jealousy. The silence. The passion. The return of jealousy. She was tiring of it. In her frustration, she looked at Alan and wondered what it would be like to sleep with him. Maybe he could set her free.

They headed toward Coolidge Corner, Brookline's urban nexus of retail stores, a movie theater, single family houses with lawns, wide streets; trees.

"Did I mention that I'm thinking of pre-med," she said, suddenly.

"I'm impressed," Alan said, staring at her. He surveyed her face, and she saw him imagining what it would be like to see her naked too.

"Depends on what day you talk to her," Kevin said. "What hour." His head turned to her now. "Finishing school would help."

"What?" she said, disbelieving.

"Let her figure out what she wants," Alan said.

"Yes, she needs to do that," Kevin said.

She sat back and thought carelessly of slipping her fingers down Alan's pants.

OAK TREES THICK as elephants lined the front walk of Michele's sorority house, a four-story mansion for music students. Inside, a clatter of shouting college kids and the stinging smell of beer greeted them. One blond boy with shoulder-length hair handed newcomers beer as they walked in.

"More to drink in the kitchen," the blond said.

Kevin went for the piano in the living room and lo and behold, there was Michele transfigured into a ravishing creature on the piano bench. Jennifer detoured in the opposite direction. The kitchen was swarming with loud-talking students. She slipped a pill into her mouth and finished her beer in two long swigs. What next? She spotted an open wine bottle next to the sink.

"Come outside with me," Alan said, pinching her waist with his hand.

She turned and he handed her a Styrofoam cup.

"Gin. It works faster," he said.

She smelled the rim of his cup and tested the liquid. He had mixed it with a dash of orange juice and it went down easily, refreshingly. She laughed, sustaining a wild, intemperate look in her eyes. On an empty stomach it didn't take long for her thoughts to jangle nonsensically.

"Come on," she said, pulling his hand toward the back door. "Let's go outside."

She took a few more steps and crossed into that timeless room where she could do anything she wanted without consequence. He followed.

In the shadows of the backyard, pine trees lacing the property appeared more distant than they actually were. The lawn, stiffened with frost, bent like thin, wire mesh under her feet. She headed for the small swing set and began to swing under a big, leafless oak. She knew it was cold but felt nothing.

"Here's to figuring out what you want," he said lifting his cup. He drank the rest and stood in front of her, catching her knees when she swung back toward him. He held her in mid-air and leaned closer to her.

She liked it, so close to his face.

"You'll be back," he said, releasing her.

The night swooned up and down, tipping and curving around a bend. She looped toward him again, then slipped off the swing and knocked against him. He caught her before she fell.

"Hello there," she said, kissing him quickly. She heard the beginning of Madonna's "Get into The Groove" playing, and beyond that, Kevin's piano and Michele's flute from inside the house.

"Let's go in," she said. She pushed toward the lighted kitchen, taking the porch steps two at a time with her long legs. The sudden heat from inside caused her to list and break into a sweat. She heard them clearly now: the intensity of the piano and flute joining, tensile and intertwining between the crowded walls.

She threaded her way to the front of the house. The largest crowd gathered in the grand foyer. She looked over and saw him hunched over the keyboard like a large bird of prey. Michele undulated to the music; her elbows spread open, lips pursed to the silver tip.

Jennifer crossed over to a vacant window seat in the hall, falling into its flowering cushion.

"Talk to me," Alan said.

She was sinking into a trash heap of bad behavior, yet the window seat felt soft as rose petals. Why leave except for the thought that Ledger's brass bed offered something even softer and otherworldly, the gentle arms of an old-fashioned room.

"Can you take me home?"

Alan returned with Jay's car keys and she went with him to the car. Outside Kevin's musical phrases dissolved behind the car glass, entered her mind and played on and on. As soon as she sat back against the seat and closed her eyes, she fell into a pool of darkness, bigger than the universe.

"Jen, we're here."

He feathered her lips with his, wakening her in front of Ledger's house. He pressed harder, then he lifted her head up and she opened her eyes. All the windows were dark. Not even the front light had been left on.

Where was Kevin? She looked at Alan and thought it would be ideal if she could have them both: Kevin's intellectual delicacy combined with Alan's muscular attitude. She felt his tongue and this put her in a sensual dream of wanting Kevin, yet aching for a thrill, daring to take what she knew she shouldn't have. She twisted into the back seat until he lay with her, his trousers snagged down where his warm legs pressed against hers, and quickly he let go inside her, collapsing against her, hunkering onto his side. She felt hot-wired, crackling before an implosion.

"I've got to go." She yanked her pantyhose up over her hips.

"Wait."

"Can't." She felt for the door handle and opened it.

"Jen – wait, please."

"I can't. Not now."

He let her go and somehow she found the key in her pocket. Ledger's door opened and she leaned into the banister in the dark, climbing away from the party confusion, pausing in front of the bathroom and sliding against the hall wall toward her room at the end.

"WHO'S THERE?" LEDGER called down from the third floor.

She swayed in the dry, silent air. She had complied with his rules. No men had come in. He ought to leave her alone. She stood still and waited, not answering, until the hall phone startled her and she tiptoed back to make it stop.

"Hello?"

'It's me," Alan said. "I called your cell but you didn't pick up. We need to talk."

"Wait." She pulled the phone into the bathroom and squeezed the door shut against the cord. "I can't talk. He's listening. How did you get this number? Don't call back. I'll call you."

She hung up and put the phone back on the hall table.

In her room, low clouds covered her in a dream. Alone on a prairie she watched a horse feed on spare grasses. She walked closer. A man appeared with a gun. He turned and smiled at her as a line of flame ignited across the horse's back.

"Shoot it," she screamed to the man. He looked at her and smiled again. "Shoot it! Can't you hear me?"

She turned onto her back and watched the burning horse evaporate into one of the flowers on the wall. The muscle over her eyebrow ached, her tongue so dry it caught in her teeth. It was too bright to see. She reached into the drawer of the nightstand and scratched the bottom for the capsules rolling to the back. A stale glass of water half-disappeared in the light.

When she awoke again, Ledger's voice downstairs came up through the radiator like a bad tape, fading and skipping words. Sentences submerged in vitriolic sounds. Later, the feeling of losing something forced her out of bed. There was work, too, in a few hours. She tightened her robe around her waist and cracked open her door just enough to peek into the hall. It was empty. She needed to call Kevin. Where was her cell phone?

In the hall, she found a cardboard box wrapped in kite string on the phone table. DO NOT USE had been marked on all four sides of the box, the phone cord disappearing into the wall like a rat's tail scurrying out of sight.

She stepped into the bathroom and locked it, dropping her robe on the toilet seat, then circling freely as the water filled the tub. At this time of day, sunlight knocked against the shiny tiles. The floor felt cool and forgiving under her feet.

If Mr. Ledger yelled at her she would dive underwater to stop him. If he couldn't get in and pounded on the door, and then said, "Open this door god damn it!" just like her father did, she would scream, "I'm not moving," and stand back brave and dripping wet in the middle of the room.

In the tub she flapped water over her skin. She rubbed away her father's verbal slaps across her cheek and arms, then dunked her head to submerge Kevin's growing disinterest.

Clean and dressed, she took a pill before preparing to leave for work. Then she sat on the bed and waited.

She waited with the patience of someone refusing to acknowledge what was falling apart around her. She'd lost her cell somewhere. What did it matter? She plucked random lint from her skirt until a feeling of reverie streamed into her blood from the pill and told herself that sometimes the world came together.

Opening her door, she smelled a cigar, a sweet sedentary odor in the hall and followed it.

"I'm on my way to work," she said standing in the older boarder's doorway. "I'm Jennifer. I live at the end." Her head tilted in the direction of her room.

"Joseph Rizzo," he said in a lumbering Italian accent. "Glad you could stop by. Where do you work?"

"I'm a server – a waitress."

He sat at a card table in front of the TV and shuffled his cards, nodding. "I was a chef once. You know the restaurant, Longines, in New York?"

She shook her head. She knew zilch about restaurants except for the one she worked in, which was a steak-and-fries, salad-and-big-drinks-place that brought in huge tips.

"I worked there twenty-three years. A very famous place. But that was a long time ago when I was young, like you. Yes, that's right." He nodded, pleased with the connection he had made between them.

"Who's the other boarder?" she asked.

"War veteran. Vietnam. He has his troubles. Drinking. As for myself, Janie – "

"Jennifer," she corrected him.

"Yes, Jennifer. Now I'm waiting for death. You see death is a hole in the ground. That's what I say." He swept his paw over the cards and reshuffled them. "That's all it is. I've a warm place to sleep, a working

TV; I enjoy the soaps and down the street they serve a nice lunch. Nice people there too. I go every day except Wednesdays. Wednesdays they're closed." He picked up his cigar and relit it.

"You're a pretty girl," he added. "You should be happy."

"You think so?"

She leaned into the threshold and smiled. "You're a very nice man."

AT THE RESTAURANT she forgot about herself and concentrated on customer orders. Rare or medium steak – free range, grain fed cows were the rave. Baked potato? Drinks? She pressed against shoulders, inched her way between perfumed blouses and ladies' soft breasts. Middle-aged couples waiting to be seated grew boisterous as the night ticked on. The restaurant didn't accept reservations so customers drank on empty stomachs. By the time they were ready to eat, the older men were drunk and talked to her as if she were their daughter or niece. Did she have a boyfriend? Many admirers? With her looks, they said, she could be a model, have her pick. The wives tolerated their husbands' seductive indulgences. It reminded them of earlier, sexier times in their married lives.

By midnight she was wide-eyed, hyper-awake, climbing imaginary rungs of hope. Afterward, she drank too many White Russians – vodka, Kahlua and cream – pooling and dividing her tips with the other servers, getting woozy again, waiting for fatigue.

She took a cab to Ledger's and climbed the stairs to her second floor, forgetting yesterday's egregious confrontation with the cardboard box, until she saw it again:

the phone tied and quartered in string. This incensed her. She would not let him do this to her. Turning, she snuck down to the first floor and used the phone in a nook under the stairs. She had given up finding her cell, convinced she lost it in Michele's backyard.

"Kevin?" she whispered when he picked up. "Ledger strung up the phone. I can't talk long. I'm sorry I left."

"I called your cell earlier. It wasn't working. What's going on Jen?"

"I was at work. If you'd come over, you'd see. Are you alone?"

"What are you doing," Ledger said. He stood midway down the staircase, a vulturous shadow in the dark.

She hung up.

"I'm coming from work."

"That phone is not for public use."

Hovering beneath the stairs, she waited for him to move. His rules were absurd. He turned and wavered upwards, around the second landing to the attic where he slept.

She stood against the wall for a long time. Her legs ached. She heard steam heat crawling up through the walls and the dead silence of sleepers. Finally, she went up to her room for another pill. It didn't take long to feel the pill's sumptuous, full-bodied embrace.

Early the next morning, she woke to the sound of furniture toppling and Ledger's voice shouting through the wall behind her headboard. When she opened her eyes again the sun flashed. She turned on her side and saw a white envelope under the door crack.

You've used two utilities at once, Ledger wrote in a script that rubbed against her fingertips like Braille. *The phone and the bathroom. Phone privileges have been taken away.*

She shredded the note, but saw shadows of feet passing her door. The unknown boarder's doorknob rattled down the hall. Someone with uneven legs stomped down the stairs. She dressed, put on her winter coat and hurried outside to walk off the absurdity of Ledger's logic, the impending disaster of her love life. But Ledger's voice nipped at her heels like her father's, until the two disciplinarians galloped in tandem, chasing her. *You've used two utilities at once. You think you have special privileges?* She circled her block imagining Kevin's apartment, walking in when he didn't answer; finding an unmade bed; the smell of recently smoked cigarettes; empty beer cans; a flute across his sheets. She wanted to call him but she knew he was at a rehearsal. She circled the block four more times and went back to the boarding house.

"A boy came by," Ledger called to her from his wing chair.

"Kevin?"

"No, his name was Alan."

She blocked the doorway.

"Mr. Ledger. If I need to make an emergency phone call, what should I do?" He took off his reading glasses.

"An emergency phone call is fine; otherwise, you may use the pay phone down the street." He slid his glasses on, jiggling them to give them a snug fit, and returned to his newspaper. The piano top gleamed in the sun. She went out again to the center of town.

Outside, the hour was slow. She was happy once wasn't she? She scanned the store fronts: the card stop where she collected trolls as a child, their bright-colored hair soft as milkweed; coke and muffins at the ice cream store. Under a cold, flat sun, she passed the town field where her mother took her and her older sister, Ruth, to play. Her sister lived in Florida now.

"Jennifer!"

She heard a loud honk and saw Alan coming toward her in a garbage cart. In the short time she had known him, he had left a job driving a bread truck and now he picked up garbage for the town – not this town, he had driven out of his territory – because the money was good.

"Kevin took off to his aunt's beach house. He knows something's up."

"How do you know this?"

"Can you get in?" Alan leaned over to open the small door. "Did the old man tell you I came by? That place is weird."

"Did you talk to Kevin?"

"Jay did. What do you want to do Jen? Kevin's not going for this one." He reached over to cup her breast but she waved him away.

"Stop. Okay? I need to think."

She crossed the street and went into a luncheonette, the one she guessed Mr. Rizzo frequented but it was too early for lunch. Inside, construction workers were fork lifting scrambled eggs and toast. She had to find her cell, but she didn't have his aunt's number. Maybe Alan had it.

In the ladies rest room, she leaned into the mirror. The muscle over her eye ached again, pulsing. Maybe her brain was eroding from her grandfather's pills, or desperation and insecurity. She had fucked up. She didn't know what to do.

"Jen?" Alan tapped on the door. "You okay in there?"

She opened the door.

"I made a mistake. We made a mistake."

He stood in front of her breathing hard. She could still smell gin.

"You're just scared."

"Kevin's your friend."

"Hey, babe. Don't' moralize with me. He's your ex-lover because it's not happening between you two. You should call Michele."

"Stop this," she said shaking her hands.

He looked at his watch. "I'll leave it up to you then."

She didn't stop him from getting back into his trash truck and pulling away. He was right and he was wrong. Across the street, a dog lifted its leg to a tree. The sky was fading behind brittle clouds. She started walking toward home.

When she opened the door to the kitchen she smelled breakfast, roasted coffee beans and toast and saw them at the kitchen table, distant as her childhood had become.

"Jennie!"

Her mother rose and came over to her, her dark eyebrows squirreling with worry.

Check me out, Jennifer wanted to say. *Take a look at your jittery pill-popping daughter.*

"You've lost weight."

"She must be hungry. That's why she came home," he said, swiping his mouth with a napkin, smoothing a crease on his suit jacket. "You don't have the decency to call and give us your address?"

"Let me get you something to eat," her mother said. Her mother wore black slacks and a beige blouse, her stay at home clothes when she wasn't volunteering at the church or hospital.

Jennifer saw the coffee pot on the countertop full of fresh, perfumed brew. She was tempted to pour some for herself.

"She wants money. Why do you think she came home?" Her father started to get up and the movement scared her. His silver hair glinted like a knife.

"I'm not hungry," she said easing away from her mother's weakened look, her impotent plea. Her mother donated time at the cancer gift shop but when it came to rescuing her from her father's violent impulses, she stood in a corner, bullied by her husband for too many years. And now here it was again, like so many times in her life; Jennie sought her mother's help, but her mother was no safer than quicksand.

She couldn't go there anymore.

She ran outside while their voices called through the rooms of her brain. *"Where's she going now? I don't know. Why didn't you tell her to stay and eat? Did you see how she looked?"* Street sign after street sign she ran until she reached the boarding house once more. Ledger was standing near the banister folding bed sheets in the upstairs hall.

"I've had trouble with him before," he said as she walked around him on the way to her room. "He lost a leg in the war but that's no excuse. He drinks. I don't allow drinking!"

The door to the unknown boarder's room had been thrust wide open, the mattress stripped to gray stripes, she saw, before she closed her own flimsy door.

Directly, she penciled a note to Ledger and dropped it on the bed.

"I used to live here," it said. And although she knew it made more sense to wait for Sunday's paper to look for a brand new place, she scooped some change from the drawer with the pills – red bullets, which she pushed away in disgust – and bought a newspaper from the machine down the street.

Next she waited for the bus on the corner. When it arrived it swept her up in the cold empty morning. The second time would be easier she decided as she moved to the back. Hadn't she already developed an aptitude for the classifieds? All those lists in black and white neatly spread across her knees. As for Kevin, he had already unlatched the gate and was diminishing. The bus surged forward and she felt her spine burning without love. Alan, she was convinced, got his kicks from the chase. So she fled as any animal would, out of instinct, toward the scent of nurturing waters and the promise of a sweet tasting hand.

Woman with Birds in her Chest

O n Thursday, ten minutes to four, Cynthia walked into her director's office at St. Agnes Hospital and submitted her resignation. She didn't want another job. She was lucky she didn't need one. Money wasn't her issue. But fifteen and a half years with the elderly had taken its toll. Old people have incurable ailments. What could she say to them about the inevitable? That aging and its related problems will go away?

"It's just time," she said to Nan, who looked up from her desk and nodded in her mild, non-confrontational way. Only Nan's double chin gave away her habit of eating too many chocolates and sweets to relieve the ongoing stress of her position. So, without trying to dissuade her, Nan asked if Cynthia would stay another month until she found someone to replace her. Of course Cynthia, who prided herself on doing everything right and correct, said she would.

During the next few weeks, Cynthia withdrew from her associates, except for Moira, who was extroverted, and a hard person to escape. Moira went after things. To the others Cynthia in her usual gracious and measured way, pulled away. In the corridors people said, "You're leaving!" and squeezed her arm as if in condolence, as if checking her blood pressure and pulse. Cynthia resented this but smiled to reassure them. No tragedy had occurred here. She was fine. Leaving was her choice.

As expected, they planned a party. On her last day, Nan gathered scores of staff who intersected with social services, a department that functioned as a catchall for every division, a medical way station for patients no matter what their disease.

Cynthia analyzed her sendoff as fulfilling a mandatory rite of closure. Administrative heads from Radiology, Cardiology, Respiratory Diseases all the way down the line of command, the pyramid of control, assistants and nursing aids wandered in and out of the conference room. Even Mrs. Jackson, Cynthia's client, was there: small and emaciated, twisting her beads, looking sad next to the oversized cake.

Public displays were distasteful to Cynthia. She attributed this to her Presbyterian upbringing and to her elderly parents who had limited energy for their only child. *Don't bother. Don't fuss*, her mother liked to say. Cynthia performed as best as she could at her afternoon *sayonara*; opening gifts, forcing a happy face – *what is that face, someone please tell* – she kept thinking as she held up two candlestick holders, a gold chain, an appointment book, and a tiny emerald pin. This was her finale, a measure of her achievement she reminded herself. Tying it all up.

Landmark. Demarcation. Crossing. *What?*

Fifteen years on the job. Fifteen years of *fill-in-the-blank* behind her.

Her replacement, a young woman named Roxanne Morgan whom Cynthia hired fresh out of graduate school, stood near the back and looked on. Good for Roxanne for knowing not to impede.

After the party, Cynthia checked her desk one last time. She didn't want Roxanne inheriting used erasers, bent paper clips. She didn't want to leave fingerprints of herself behind. Roxanne had a Master's degree, like Cynthia, but Cynthia had the immeasurable experience. Roxanne would have to make her own way.

After the party, Moira was called to another floor on an emergency admission. Nan lingered and watched Cynthia walk out of St. Agnes' for good. It was cold outside in this Northeastern city, a streak of pink zigzagging across the darkening sky as she stood on the icy pavement in her low heels until someone honked, another well wisher, waving bye. Startled, Cynthia hurried to her car.

The first weeks at home she slept late and read magazines in bed. Her husband, Miles, didn't say anything. He said she deserved the rest. "You do what you want," he said.

But she didn't need his permission.

"I don't mean it that way," he said apologetically.

She spent a week indulging herself at the malls, succumbing to a buying spree. She bought practical navy pumps, slacks lined with slippery black taffeta. A jewelry store caught her eye. So much hope in those glittering stones, those ancient histories of light. She bought a diamond pendant and hid it in her jewelry box. *From whom was she hiding*? She wondered. Miles would not have protested her expensive purchase.

She considered taking a Spanish class but stopped herself. Once she visited Miles in his office. *What a silly idea*. Her husband was an internist with a subspecialty in renal disorders. His patients were elderly too. His beeper went off continually. Complaints; worried faces. *Oh, hadn't she just escaped this? Dumb, dumb, dumb.* Miles looked kindly at her. There was nothing he could do to stop the flow of others' needs.

"See you at home," he said.

In April she struggled in her sleep. Her dreams became shadows of fingers, and the night, a troubling piece of lint in her throat. Beside her Miles slept with his arm heavy on her thigh. She wanted to wake him. *Something wrong? Everything okay?* he would have asked. But she didn't.

She didn't know. She didn't know.

In the morning, she stared into the closet at her white cotton robe hanging there. *Such a simple thing.* It's hard to figure what's missing sometimes.

Other nights she sat up with her knees pulled to her chest as if she hurt. But she felt nothing. She listened to Miles quietly breathing.

June mornings, the sun shone off the white stove, white tiled floor, white countertops. Until she quit her job, she never knew there were so many hours in a solitary day.

Mrs. Jackson, her former client, knew. Mrs. Jackson said hours didn't exist for counting time; they measured events. Every Tuesday when she came to see Cynthia, she wore the same black knit dress, the same grouping of chains around her neck, the same red scarf to hold back her hair. "You're too young to understand, dear," she said, fondling her chains.

Loneliness was in Mrs. Jackson's shoulders, her throat, the joints in her knees, her sciatica nerve and intestinal tract. Cynthia listened and recommended x-rays, Kaopectate, traction, Prednisone. None of these remedies worked.

One morning in July, Miles turned to her in the kitchen. He held a mug of coffee in one hand, a croissant in the other. "You're bored. You're getting depressed," he said. "You need a change."

She heard what he said but she *couldn't explain it.* She developed pains in her chest. *Breathing in out in out.*

After the hot sun in August slipped across the kitchen floor, she moved to the couch in the den and sat, legs knotted, studying patterns in the rug. *If she could find the answer.* The air conditioner chugged in the window behind her. She pulled at the skin on her neck to open her throat for air. *What good was breathing?* It was hard getting air, like birds flying in her chest, their wings caught in her ribs.

Were there no true answers to behold in this life?

Years ago, when Miles was a resident at St. Agnes', they found each other and discovered that they both grew up in small, rural towns. They both attended state colleges and shared an interest in health care. Miles was an only child, too.

During one of their coffee breaks, talking over the pink speckled tables in the cafeteria, Miles asked her to marry him. They had a short engagement, a tiny ceremony. His mother, her parents, Miles' best friend and Cynthia's aunt attended. Happy? Was she *happy?*

She thought so.

Trudging back upstairs through the hallway of her lovely stucco home, she lay down to consider happiness, pulling their coverlet over her shoulders, she dreamed *in the shadow of the pillow, meteorites the*

*size of her fist falling from the sky in a nameless town
in a nameless world. People she didn't know came out
of their homes to watch. When the stones broke against
the ground, butterflies flew out. She ran and stumbled
on a rock shining bright as a prayer at her feet and knelt
down to inspect it.*

The sound of a shrill ringing woke her. She reached for
the telephone on the night table and heard Moira's voice.

"Hi there stranger! Where in the world have you gone?"

"I'm here."

"Are you sick?" she asked. "What's wrong? You
sound funny."

"Nothing, why?" Cynthia sat up and cleared her throat.

"You sound different."

MOIRA INSISTED ON lunch. Five days later, Cynthia
stood in front of her bedroom mirror ironing her long
skirt with her hands, fixing the collar of her gray silk
blouse. She turned and twisted in her new pumps, dissat-
isfied with her hair, which was short and tucked behind
her ears.

"This is my treat," Moira said greeting her in the restaurant. Moira had a small waist, full breasts and hips; a
model's flawless complexion. She wore necklines offering
up cleavage that Cynthia thought inappropriate at work.
But somehow, in a way that Cynthia couldn't understand,
Moira simply got away with it.

"You will not believe what's been happening," Moira
said, steering her over to a booth she had already saved
for them. "Mrs. Jackson moved in with a man – don't
even ask – he's seventy-eight – and no, they're not married. She met him at one of the group sessions."

"What group sessions?"

"Your successor has come up with a good idea," she said, "but let's order first. I'm starved."

The red vinyl-lined seat hissed when Cynthia sat down.

"It's all working out, thanks to you," she added. "I mean, you picked her."

Cynthia opened the menu and read down an encyclopedic list of entrees, drinks, desserts, but couldn't make up her mind.

"I don't know what to choose."

"Don't hold back."

"Soup," Cynthia said to the young man waiting for their orders. He looked college-bound, ready to ride all the humps and bumps of life. She handed him the menu.

"That's all?" Moira said. "I'll have the seafood platter and a glass of milk."

"I'm glad all is well," Cynthia said, though something small and dark in her mind had hoped that things might fall apart in her absence. She admonished herself for this evil, untidy thought.

"Yes, but you've lost weight," Moira said. "Have you been running? What have you been doing? We haven't heard a peep in *months*."

Cynthia shrugged. "Taking time, I guess."

"Well, I have something to tell you. I'm pregnant. Four months already. I'm taking a leave at eight months. Believe me, I'm already counting the days – one hundred and eighteen days left."

The college kid returned. He placed a bowl of vegetable soup in front of Cynthia and warned her not to burn her tongue. Then he left again.

"Go on, silly. Get started," Moira said.

"Wonderful news," Cynthia said, not feeling a thing. That made her feel even stranger, so she picked up her spoon and tried to eat.

The waiter came back with Moira's platter.

"Oooh. Look at this. How's your soup? All I want to do is chow down all day." Moira launched into her shrimp.

"Tell me about those sessions," Cynthia said, though in truth she wanted to go back home, *like an invalid who has fallen in love with her bed.*

"It started with coffee and cake," Moira said, laughing. "That got everybody to show up.

"Food's a wonderful equalizer." Cynthia heard herself speaking mechanically and hated herself for it.

"Yep. Sure is." Moira plowed a forkful of shrimp into her mouth and chewed vigorously. "Each week we have a topic. Last week, ten people showed up and talked about how they felt when they woke up in the morning; what went through their heads. It sounds simplistic. But it's not really," she said, swallowing. "The new you – Roxie we call her – digs for details. A person can't just say, 'lousy' or 'depressed'. Roxie tells them to go back to a specific moment of waking and describe smells, sounds, feelings. You should hear how they talk."

She stopped to wipe her fingers. "Now we're planning a field trip. Bird watching. You should come. Mrs. Jackson is always asking about you. We all wonder what you've been doing and why you haven't called. It's like you disappeared. You probably want to forget St. Agnes' existence ... "

ON THE RIDE back Cynthia thought how she had never desired children, and luckily, neither had Miles.

But such a decision put her outside the ring of normal. People questioned it. Others assumed she had tried and failed and when they learned she hadn't even tried, they secretly suspected that she had some aberrant, twisted reason for not choosing that path.

It's worth it, a parent will say. Of course her parents were disappointed. But, in her opinion, too many so-called parents in this world had no clue about how to nurture, and were never called to task for the mistreatment of their children. In Cynthia's case, she was simply ignored.

As a child, she took care of her father, who was on disability most of his adult working life. He was asthmatic and overweight. He had an injured back. Mother worked for an insurance company. When her mother retired, her parents moved away to a retirement community in North Carolina. Cynthia rarely saw them.

After her lunch with Moira, she realized that it was time to do something. She called the director of Open Arms, a hospice program in western Massachusetts that she knew about, and expressed an interest in volunteering there.

"I don't know Cynthia," Miles said to her the morning of the appointment. He shook his head. "You'll end up in the same rut. Do something *for yourself.*"

"I am. This is it." She had a stubborn streak and there was nothing he could say that would change her mind at this point. She got in the car and drove a good hour's ride to Berkshire Valley Open Arms.

The hospital was brand new, a tinted-glass encased rectangle that jutted out of a dip in the land like a dark, shiny rock. White cumulus clouds reflected off the façade. The sight reminded her of her dream and convinced her it was her fate to be here.

Inside, the director, a petite, blond woman named Kate, met her at the front desk. Kate moved slowly, patiently guiding Cynthia around corners and smiling when Cynthia thanked her for holding open the door. Everyone seemed to glide around this place. Sounds sunk back into low-lit places.

As soon as Cynthia sat down in Kate's office, Kate's phone rang.

Once again, someone was desperate. Cynthia crossed her legs and waited a long time for Kate to end the conversation. But Kate exhibited the same slow, methodical manner of speaking as she did leading Cynthia through the hallway maze. Kate kept nodding and saying, *I know, I know, I'm so sorry* –

Little dark thoughts began to pinch at her brain again. Cynthia began to feel Kate's consideration for the person on the phone was bordering on rudeness toward her who had, after all, come all this way to talk at this specific time. Kate finally hung up.

"Tell me. Why are you here?"

Why? Cynthia told her about her long, invaluable service at St. Agnes'. She talked about health care. She told Kate she missed working with people who needed her. But that was a lie. Wasn't it? Did Kate know this? She saw the director staring at her, watching intently. Did she know?

"It's rewarding yes," Kate said, who went on to say that there were all kinds of rewarding work. She said many people left before the training period ended. "Working with people who are dying is difficult," she said. "It's a terrible strain."

"Working with the elderly wasn't easy," Cynthia reminded her. Here she was trying to tell Kate something and somehow not getting through.

"We have young adults here, too. Dying comes in every form and color."

"I'd like to try."

"Yes. It's all we can do." She leaned forward and touched Cynthia's arm. "Will you join me for lunch?"

The cafeteria was walled in glass and looked like a restaurant with booths and round tables and plants. There were stations for salads and homemade soups. Thinking of Moira, she chose the seafood salad. Kate stirred her clam chowder, dipping the spoon in the milky paste, stirring round and round as she talked. She told Cynthia that her husband died of a rare nerve disorder. "Upstairs in this place," she said, raising her eyes. "And here I am. Five years later. I find it comforting. What about you? Who have you lost?"

Lost?

"No one." She felt stupid and exposed, as if she had just confessed a major failure in her life. "Well, no one besides a grandparent," she added. "My grandmother died of a stroke. She was eighty-nine."

Kate stopped her stirring and looked at her. How old was she when her grandmother died? Did she cry? Did Cynthia feel 'right' about it? What were her feelings at the time?

Feelings? Right?

No. she hadn't cried, Cynthia told her.

"I saw the distress it caused my mother. My mother and grandmother had been very close. I was in college at the time. But my grandmother lived far away in Florida, where she had moved eight years before. I didn't know her very well. It was my mother who needed the comfort."

Kate nodded and smiled oddly. "Ah, I see you were the caretaking child."

"Yes. I suppose so."

For three weeks after that, Cynthia handed out magazines and made herself available to anyone who needed to talk.

"Who are you helping?" Miles asked after they settled in at a table in a small, French bistro that had opened up in their suburb. They had just seen a movie about missing children in Argentina. "I thought you wanted to take some courses. What about those Spanish lessons you talked about?" The waiter had taken their orders and was filling their glasses with red wine.

"They need me."

"I'm worried about you."

"I like it," she said, evading his point. "I'm there for them."

The September night was mild. After a dinner of fish smothered in lentils, they strolled along the back streets. Newton was a family town, a child-centered town filled with doctors and lawyers and overzealous democrats. They walked by a family of five laughing loudly, slurping on ice cream cones.

"You need them more than they need you," he said, bringing up the subject again.

At forty-nine years old, her husband had a flat, sturdy brow and strong hands. Miles' hair was thinning, even starting to gray. *Strange how it comes to us, this slow dying,* Cynthia thought.

"What do you mean by that?" she stopped and turned toward him.

"It takes you away from yourself; their pain takes over."

"No. It brings me closer. Death tells me who I am."

"How does it do that?"

"It's like a mirror. It forces you to look at yourself, strip away the lies."

"Life can do that too."

"I don't see how," she said.

"I know. That's my point. Well, I don't want to argue about it," he said, turning in the direction of their parked car.

She didn't either. That was not something they did.

At Open Arms, Cynthia met Brooke, who was forty-one and married like Cynthia. Brooke spent four years on fertility drugs to produce a child. Now she anguished over whether those same drugs had caused her breast cancer.

"You bore a beautiful child," Cynthia said on one of her afternoon visits. Greeting cards papered the wall above Brooke's bed and on her bedside table: photos of her husband, a lean, wide-shouldered man, and many snapshots of her red-cheeked, toddler.

Brooke lay on her bed with eyes closed, apparently sleeping. The anti-cancer drugs had pummeled her organs, causing a kidney shut down. When a tumor showed up in her lungs, Brooke came to Open Arms. Her bald head was smooth as a bird's egg, her wrists stripped down to the bone.

"Brooke. How are you today?" Cynthia asked, sitting in a chair beside her. She thought she'd heard Brooke whisper something and stop. Cynthia leaned closer to listen. The other day, she thought Brooke had stopped breathing, and then her breast sunk in and she gasped another breath. Cynthia waited for her to breathe again.

"I'm here, Brooke. What is it?"

She thought she heard a gurgling sound in Brooke's throat. A dribble of saliva sputtered. She couldn't remember how long it was before another volunteer walked in and ushered Cynthia out.

Kate handed her a glass of water and sat beside her in her office.

"It's your first time. Don't suppress it," she said. "Why don't you go home now. Take care of you."

Cynthia wandered outside to the crowded parking lot dazed by this swift ending to Brooke's life. When she got home, she walked into the kitchen, slid down the refrigerator door and sat on the floor. It grew dark. She heard Miles' car settle into the garage, then silence, and his steps up the back stairs.

"What are you doing on the floor?" he asked. "You need a break from this." He bent down next to her. She smelled his weakened cologne, a limey odor coming from his neck.

"I'm not important."

"Yes, you are."

He slipped down to the floor beside her and held her hand, watching her closely.

"No. Never mind. Don't bother with me," she said. "I'm sorry."

"For what? You're upset." He took her other hand.

"I'm just so sad." *So sad.*

"I know you are. Allow yourself to feel it. It's good for your heart."

"What? How will that help?" *Help!* "I've ruined everything."

"No, you haven't."

"No job. I have nothing. No life." Something inside her began riding down a current. It rocked her side to side, jarring her brain, her breath clawing its way out of some insidious womb expanding inside her. She leaned against him.

"You have *you*." He spoke gently, cradling her shoulders. "And me. Cynthia, *please*. Let your guard down. Let me in."

"How?" *How?* She heard Mrs. Jackson: *you don't count time in years, dear, you count events; that's how it is.* You know, if only she could mark this event, sliding down his torso, curling now onto the floor, the cool floor so smooth upon her cheek and bone, her chin catching a piece of grit not swept up, like gristle, like sand, like golden flecks dazzling her mind across this linoleum floor, circling, spinning, becoming swirls of cold sparks spinning against stone, she would crawl into it. "Oh my god." *God. God. She would crawl into it. Take me. Please dear God.* She heaved another breath, scrabbling toward somewhere without gravity; it had to exist, that heavenly place –

Recovery

I saw the hands on the clock some time ago – two sticks bobbing past my canoe. For on that strange lake I forgot minutes and directions and fixed my eyes on the objects that surrounded me: bedpan, thermometer, blanket, TV. During that week, I clung to those things as part of who I was while countless nurses, doctors and aides stood by me to monitor my pulse.

By the second day I had grown used to the damp feeling in my limbs. Plastic tubing, inserted in my leg and connected to a bottle outside my room, drew liquid into my bloodstream. I felt the chill of it in my bones and curled up to stop my knees from shaking. I waited for the bad weather to go away. Beside me the phone was still. I had asked my friends not to call. Their voices had no meaning for me then. I waited. My canoe spun in its course and moved on.

"You're doing fine," the nurse said. "You just sleep."

She took my arm and wound the pressure gauge around it. Afterward I felt my heart relax as the hisses from the air pump released its grip on me. But night accelerated the swirling inside. I had to push myself up, lean over the unsteady edge and expel what was left in my stomach. It spewed out effortlessly, yet it was quiet. Just my bed squeaked when I heaved nothing into the metal tin. I didn't fight it. Repeatedly I pressed my palms against the sheet and pushed my stomach to my throat before falling back.

"What do you need, El?" the nurse asked.

She had a name. Rose.

"Another tin; some water."

"Hand me what you got," she said.

My gut in a tin; she took everything and didn't seem to mind.

"Keep it up, El. You're doing great. Sleep."

I waited for morning. It was a long way down my brain. I held onto the bedrails for cold comfort, waited there and listened to the rumblings under my skin.

There was a grey light in the room on the fourth day. We kept the overhead lights off. Rose held my bare leg and I tried to sit as she ran a cloth over my skin. My thoughts were simple, the same thoughts. I'm cold. This bath is cold. I'm cold.

Finally, I lay back on a clean sheet in a clean cotton gown. Rose gone, I watched images on the TV move above me the way light moves inside my eyes when I shut them. The screen wrinkled and talked. I floated uncomfortably in space.

"Where do you ache, Elizabeth?" the doctor wanted to know. He stood outside the transparent curtain and waited for me to respond. I liked him. I was glad he was there.

"All over, like the flu."

"Serum sickness," he said. "That's a common reaction."

He walked out of my small radius of vision. Faces came and went above me. The hands on the clock on the wall opposite me pointed one way, then another. I saw things from underwater, my canoe flooded and useless. Sound and light hurt.

"But I can't see," my mouth echoed.

"That will go away," he said. "We think it's the Procarbozine. Give it a few days."

I shifted and saw a shadow that was his head and something white holding up the shadow. My grandmother was blind in her final years, but I was not an old woman.

On the sixth night the light shone in my room like sun off a snow bank. My liquid self hardened, the shape of me snow granules packed into flesh. When I moved I felt particles rearranging to fit the bed.

Rose came in and sat in a chair next to me. She wore multiple masks and gowns. Her body was blue and her face, brown. Air vents behind me blew filtered air out the door.

"Dr. Roberts isn't here yet," she said.

"What's the problem?"

"He'll be here, don't worry."

She took my blood pressure and wrote it down.

"I'm going to do this every fifteen minutes while the drug is being infused," she said. "Then every thirty minutes until midnight. It's seven-thirty now."

"Just let me know when it's over, please."

"THE TRAFFIC WAS bad," he said when he came up to the curtain.

"But you're late," I said. "Rose, are you here?"

"I'm coming in right now."

I heard her in the chair.

"Okay, we're going to start now, Elizabeth," he said.

"Sing to me, will you?" I asked.

As the Nembutal took effect, sound was an elastic pulling at my ears. I struggled with it. The ventilators behind me hummed louder until my existence was humming. Someone singing petered away. I circled inside a large tunnel vibrating with sound until it deafened all other sounds. The tunnel filled with water and sloshed me against myself. I bumped against the curving sides. It was dark. Quiet.

"The infusion's over, Liz, and you're doing fine," Rose said. "Honey, you're a trooper. That was your last dose. You're done."

IT WAS THE small things: the way the pillow held my head, the layers of blankets covering me, the ease with which I could reach the bedpan before soiling myself. On the seventh day the chemotherapy eked out of me, a human sponge drying out, my bones evacuated. Everything converged through a second tube connecting between my legs to a bag on the floor outside my room.

On the eighth day he walked up to the curtain and held my life in two bags, one in each hand. He held them as a hunter holds his prize: freshly harvested bone marrow from my brother's hip. He attached the red stuff to the tube in my leg and nodded. My vision was clearing. I saw his eyes pause like birds after a long flight. Mom and Dad hovered next to each other and my brother called to me as a nurse rolled him back to his room. He was sore and happy. It took four hours for life to inch its way back to me.

• • •

I GRIPPED THE creases of the curtain and knelt on the bed. My brother stood on the other side bending slightly at the waist. His hips were bound with surgical tape.

"You're wired up, Liz."

"I can't stay in here."

"Keep talking – talk to me."

I walked to the opposite wall of the room and looked at him through the plastic barrier.

"Come back over here," he said. "I'll give you a backrub."

He fit his hands in the rubber gloves that were attached to the curtain. I got on the bed and sat with my back facing him. He pressed his hands against my shoulders but it wasn't a hand, it was the texture of rubber. I asked him to stop. I stood up. I went to the other side of the room three steps away. I walked back to the bed and sat down. I got up. "Rose!" I heard myself shout.

"What is it, El. What's going on?" She stood at the curtain.

"I don't know. I can't stay in here. I want out."

"El, you've got to relax."

I watched her features change shape as she pressed her face against the plastic.

"You're wound up from the chemo and the transplant. I can get you a sleeping pill."

"No. I don't want one."

"But it would help. You need to sleep."

"I'm not making any sense. My head is expanding. Am I making sense?"

"Yes, Liz," Dave said. "You're doing okay."

"But where's Roberts?"

"El. It's after midnight. He's home. You need to sleep," she said again. "What can we do?"

"Get me out of here."

I looked at them both standing freely outside the curtain. Frantically, I scanned all the walls holding me in.

"Liz, come back over here," Dave urged.

"What?"

He had his hands in the gloves.

"Come here and give me a hug."

I held my arms at my side and let him wrap the rubber gloves around my shoulders. The gloves were warm from his hands. I felt layers of ice starting to thaw, the obstruction in my stomach loosening.

"Cry, Liz."

"I can't."

"Let it go."

"Let it go," he said again.

I pulled at it, wrenching, uprooting a block that was cold and hard.

"Let it go," he said, his voice quieter than before. "We're all here."

THE NEXT MORNING Roberts sat in a chair and looked at me through the curtain. I was eating a plateful of scrambled eggs, bite after bite.

"I'm better today," I said.

"Good. Do you want to tell me about it?"

"Well, there's nothing to say. I was out of it."

"Yes, I know."

He leaned back and crossed his legs. I tapped my fork on the plate.

"Who told you?"

"I know everything that goes on in here and with you."

"It's being here I suppose and those drugs. Anyway, it won't happen again. Sorry."

"Don't be. There's nothing to be sorry about. I'd be surprised if you didn't feel that way."

He watched me tear off pieces of toast into uneven shapes.

"And there's the letdown," he added.

A decline, I thought.

"Well, the worst is over," I said.

"Step one is over."

"That's great," I said, pushing the tray away from me. I stared at my blanket-covered knees. "Must you be so negative?"

"I'm being realistic, Elizabeth."

"Negative. Say something good before you leave." I looked at him and waited. He stood and leaned toward the curtain.

"You got through chemo and you're eating," he said. "That's a lot."

"Thanks."

I turned my back and heard him walking away.

"Elizabeth," he called from the outer door. "I'll talk to you later."

I switched on the television.

"Bermuda!" the announcer said.

A panorama of ocean, white sand and sun burst apart in front of me. It was Christmas time and cold where I was. Everyone said I was lucky to be inside. Snow was expected but even so there would be no way I could know except from outsiders' reports or the news. There were no windows in my room. I pressed the remote control button and watched stations spin around, past Bermuda again, until I shut it off. The second hand calmly made its way around the clock. It reminded me of second grade. Instead of listening to the teacher talk, I would stare at the clock above her head until the minute hand flinched toward the next number. Those movements, I had thought, were signs of God.

Every day Rose entered the anteroom and dressed in sterile gowns so as not to infect me when she came into my bacteria-free space. I stayed on the bed, and followed her activities: washing the walls, the chair, the plastic curtain and finally, me.

"Don't be slow now," she said. "I'm in a rotten mood and if you don't behave, I won't be kind."

"Scare me," I said. "What happened? Did you see Leroy last night?"

"All night, and it's always the same. He loves me but he won't marry me. He doesn't want me to leave," she said as she tossed the worn pillowcase out the door, "but he doesn't want to get tied down."

"Makes a lot of sense," I said, snorting.

She handed me a wet cloth. I ran it up my legs, rinsed it out, threw the cloth in a basin, took another clean cloth, dunked it in sterile cleansing solution, ran the cloth across one arm, threw the cloth in the basin, took a clean cloth, ran it along the other arm until I had used 17 washcloths to clean myself.

"Bend your head," she said.

I obeyed and let her pour a basin of the solution through my hair. I rubbed my scalp but as I lathered the soap, clumps of hair stuck to my hands.

"My God, Rose."

"Don't do that. Throw it out, Jesus. I hate to see that but it happens every time."

"I've got to look," I said. "I've got to see the mirror."

"Honey, you're gonna be here for a while. The mirror's where it always is."

I slipped on a fresh nightgown and pulled the mirror out of the utility table. My hair was thinning. In a few days, just as the doctors had warned me, my entire head would be bald.

"So what will you do?" I said as I stared at myself, tilting my head this way and that.

"I think I'll marry Ken."

"What do you mean, Ken?"

"Ken wants to marry me. He has money and a good job."

I closed the tabletop and looked at her. She had two blue masks over her face but it was easy to read her eyes.

"You're not in love with him."

"He's very nice."

"Nice, Rose."

"Honey, I'm tired. I raised four kids on my own, and lady I've got an itch behind this mask that I can't scratch. You've got me talking too much."

She gathered up the basin full of wet facecloths and stepped out of my room. It was almost time for lunch. Afterward, I would nap, later eat dinner and then Dr. Roberts would stop by before going home. I'd watch some more TV and sleep.

Nighttime. The big lake was flat. I drifted on it, gliding on the surface at peace. The horizon curved fifteen years back in memory. I was ten on an overnight trip at summer camp. My two friends and I knelt by the water's edge and made silent wishes. I prayed for my own happiness and for happiness in the world. Homemade roof-shingle boats the size of our hands floated next to our knees. Each boat balanced a candle that had been melted onto it. There was a large half-moon over the middle of the lake and on the opposite shore, someone's living room shone through the pine trees. We wondered who lived there. Did they see us the way we saw them? One of the counselors rang a small bell. The whole group, forty-one of us, leaned forward and pushed our lighted boats toward the center. The current carried them toward the left bend and it seemed as if stars had fallen and reemerged in a water-sky.

When we awoke the next morning, the moon looked like a cloud. I was late for swimming class, but as I ran from my cabin to the dock I saw a shingle boat, candleless, caught in the foam near the reeds where we never swam. The sun was white and gave off a crisp, practical light. I flung my arms straight above me, dove into the water and when I resurfaced, sat up in bed and stared at the floor.

The linoleum tiles were speckled. I wore Styrofoam slippers to protect my feet from germs. In the evening I got up and walked eight feet from one wall to the other, eight steps from one wall to the other. I circled the square tiles searching for anything that moved in my mind that would lead me somewhere. I circled and listened. I learned the songs on the radio. I watched a show about galaxies. Time towed me in and out of myself, a tireless current in my brain.

One afternoon Rose ushered a woman up to my curtain.

"This is Celine," she said. "She doesn't speak English. She's French and she has what you had. I told her you'd talk to her."

Celine looked old and young at the same time. Her clothing emphasized mature breasts and hips yet she wore red ribbons in her hair. The ribbons shook when she laughed. We stared at each other through the plastic. I pointed to my bald head and we laughed.

"It'll come back," I told her in French.

"I don't want this," she said.

I struggled to remember her language though the instant familiarity we felt didn't require words.

"Neither did I."

Her husband came up behind her and wrapped his hairy arm around her waist. They kissed without embarrassment. She told him about my hair, pointing to my head as he listened and smiled.

"Thank you," she said in English. "I'm glad you are here."

They walked out arm in arm.

I didn't see her again until the afternoon she was admitted to her transplant room next door to me. Her husband stayed until evening and stopped by my curtain before he left.

"My wife is glad you are here," he said, chewing on the "r" the way Celine did. He pointed again to my head.

"It comes back." I said, nodding to reassure him.

After he left, I could hear the television in Celine's room. Over the next several days I would hear it running all day and night. The nurses whispered a lot outside her door and Roberts no longer stopped by my room three times a day but came only once at night.

"Well, how is she? What's going on?" I asked Rose the moment she walked into my room for my morning bath.

"Okay."

"The details, Rose."

"She's having trouble. Turn the radio on will you?"

I got off the bed.

"What trouble?"

"Some kind of pain, El. We don't know what it is."

She filled the washbasin and stood back to watch me.

"When you get off those pills, you'll lose that ring around your hips."

"What kind of pain?"

"We don't know. We had to stop the treatment."

We turned to watch a technician roll a machine toward Celine's room, the machine so large it barely fit through the doorway and knocked against a wall.

"Rose."

"They're probably taking an X-ray. She's got some fluid in her chest."

"I can't take this. Where's Roberts?"

"Sit down, Liz."

"I can't. The damn bed's dirty."

"Listen to me."

She held the basin in her arms. A wet cloth dangled from her gloved hand.

"There's nothing any of us can do except wait and hope her body recovers."

"Hand me that cloth please," I said.

I washed quickly, methodically casting off one cloth after another, paying too much attention to each limb as I dried off.

The next morning I awoke early from the sound of Celine crying. It was muffled because of the air vents but persistent. I pushed the call button. A nurse I didn't know appeared in the dark.

"Can someone stay here with me?"

"We really can't, Elizabeth. We're short-staffed. I'm filling in from another floor."

"Well, I've got to see someone. Who else is out there?"

Minutes later, Roberts came through the door and up to the curtain. He hesitated.

"Your counts are going up, Elizabeth. I doubt you'll be needing any more transfusions."

"But is she going to be okay?"

I listened but I couldn't hear.

He was slow in answering then shook his head. I got up and put on my green slippers.

It was a summer day. I was older. Thirteen. Eight of us rode in the back of a pickup truck down a winding dirt road. All summer we had been swimming between docks to strengthen our bodies for lifesaving. Now we headed toward the big lake to be tested. The truck jostled our bare legs and we held on to the sides while dust formed spinnakers in the air. We talked to calm ourselves, but when a rock hit the floorboard we grew silent. Pebbles shattered the fenders as we came upon the clearing. Then the truck stopped. We hopped out, pulled off our T-shirts, and lined up along the shore. Three counselors swam out shouting instructions. I waited for the whistle and ran in.

I breaststroked out, pushing water away, then dove to the bottom and secured my hand around the submerged counselor's chin. I ignored my need for air. Her golden hair floated downward as I pulled her up to the surface and quietly toward shore.

Second whistle. Three more girls dove into the water. I sat cross-legged, my skin red and dripping. Someone several yards out began to thrash. We heard gulping sounds, gasps. One of the counselors emerged with an arm around Jennie, the shy girl in our class, and carried her in.

The rest of us knelt a small distance away while Jennie shook in the sand. The head counselor told her that she was okay, that she had hyperventilated from nerves. "We'll go on from here, girls," she called back to us. "We've got a schedule to keep. Who's up next? Let's go!" She stood and clapped her hands. We ran to our places.

Whistle. I knew I was swimming. The woman ahead of me was flailing her arms, kicking. I dove under and grabbed her legs. One hand over the other I climbed her body, planting hand on knee, hip, armpit, pulling her back against my chest until her whole side pressed against mine. She struggled to break free. I tightened my arms in a vice around her and held her mercilessly until my knees scraped sand. We stood up panting. I felt my strength rise up.

"Do you want your lunch now, Liz?"

The dietician standing at the doorway held her arm out waiting to pass me a tray.

IN THE EVENING a man came in with the X-ray machine and heaved it toward Celine's door. The sound of the electrocardiograph raced through the wall that divided our two rooms. A woman's voice kept repeating the same words from a loudspeaker in the hallway. People crowded into the anteroom. I switched on the TV. Rose came and stood by my curtain. Celine's heart had swollen to the size of a football, Rose would later say. When Roberts stepped out of Celine's room, his shoulders folded in on themselves. Doctors I didn't recognize walked in slow circles. Later, someone came and wheeled a sheet-covered body away.

Over the weeks that followed, I stood at the door of my room and counted the boxes of needles and towels stacked against the far wall or spun the TV stations out of habit. I knitted a scarf for my brother and rolled the last paper days of the calendar into weightless balls.

Shoreline

In the morning I threw Jim's pillow out the window. It flies like a white bird plummeting. The phone rings and rings, that's all I can remember. Oh, yes. The clothes. Before I left, I kicked the bedroom closet door and took my clothes.

I met my husband on a summer evening five years ago at a post-graduation party in Weston, Massachusetts. It was one of those parties you hear about from a friend who heard about it from another friend of another friend. I didn't know the people who owned the big house and the bigger backyard where the party took place, in the neighborhood where the streets flowed up and down like ocean swells, and the trees along the streets were so old and mature they dwarfed the estate-sized houses beneath them. I drove to the party alone. I had my liberal arts degree rolled up in its cardboard tube in the car trunk, but I was one of those people who didn't know what they wanted to do after college except get a job, make money, fall in love.

So I got the job at a realty office, which promised big money if I worked hard enough. I got the one bedroom apartment in Brookline and, as for love, well, the party took place on a flagstone terrace behind the house.

Bug repellant candles surrounded the pool and had been placed strategically in the darkest corners of the backyard. A tall, slender man with bright dark eyes came up to me. He had a job, too, in engineering. What was I planning to do with my life? he asked me.

"I haven't planned that far in advance."

"I want to make a lot of money," he said. "Buy a big house, furnish it with English and French provincial furniture, and the best stereo equipment available. The best of everything," he assured me. "Later on, have three kids."

"Three?"

"Absolutely. Three."

"You're very sure about everything," I said. "I don't know how many I want. I don't know if I want any at all."

"You will,' he said. "Everyone wants kids."

"No," I said. "No, they don't."

Sometime after midnight, he and I left the party and walked under those enormous trees. I wore a dress with spaghetti straps that slipped off my shoulder with every laughing breath. I had my black hair tied back in a clip. The next night he picked me up at my apartment and took me to dinner in the Italian North End. I ate in a restaurant with whitewashed plaster walls that made my dark hair look darker, my tanned skin tinted rose like the wine that I drank. On the way home, he undressed me in the bucket seat. I sank into the softest leather.

At the wedding, seven months later, I wore a taffeta dress, strapless this time. Two hundred people came to the Cape Cod estate that had been restored for public celebrations. Jim's family paid for half. After the wedding, a limo took us to the airport and we got our connecting flight to Hawaii. It seemed everything in

Hawaii smelled sweet. Candle-white flowers bloomed everywhere. I mean everywhere.

I moved right in to this rental cottage by the sea; have run every morning since.

Soon after, Jim started an engineering company and I began selling houses in the suburbs of Boston. I worked late. He worked later. We bought a contractor's spec house. Everything had a five-year warranty sticker: the washing machine, the dryer, the fridge, the kitchen cupboards guaranteed for life. Jim wired up an intercom and hi-fi system. I ordered furniture from catalogues. Every night we saw each other in the king-sized bed. Pillows and quilts smothered us. I wore long, diaphanous things. We swam across cotton flowered sheets.

I do my warm up stretching first, surveying the two tiny rooms inside, hands splayed like starfish, bare toes curled on the warped wooden floor. My bras hang on the door-knobs; my camisoles cling to the kitchen cupboard handles. I twist my twenty-six-year-old body up and down, back and around, then push open the screen door and cross the dunes to the sandy beach below.

Sometime during the second year of our marriage, in the fall, Jim opened another division and got home later and later until I didn't know when he got into bed. I had already fallen asleep under the spell of our sweet smelling quilt, late night TV on, talking to me. The refrigerator stayed empty except for leftover Chinese food in cartons I took home after work. I was too tired to cook. I had a clientele following by then, couples whose worries grew tenfold times ten.

"We got divorced after we built the dream house," one woman with two children confided to me. "After twenty-five years."

I had run an ad for a rental house. The woman met me outside the front door. She was a small, grey-skinned woman who looked older than her age, bitten too many times, it seemed, by loneliness.

"See," she went on to explain in the eat-in kitchen I showed her, a center hall colonial with four bedrooms, three baths. "My ex and I spent so much time on the house. It took three years to build. We were trying to build a dream that didn't exist between us. Once the house was finished, there was nothing left."

I thought the story unusual until I heard another one dangerously like it a few weeks later. This time my confessor had blond hair, looked my age, and talked out the window as I drove slowly around curving streets.

"We renovated the entire house," she told me. "Attic to basement, back porch to master bedroom suite – oh look at that," she said, pointing to a brick house similar to the one she was leaving.

"That'll make a good price comparison," I said. "We'll look at it the next time."

"Well, anyway," she said. "As soon as the last nail had been driven into the molding, he left me for another woman. I had absolutely no idea."

I shook my head. "Nightmare."

Later that day she sat at my desk, legs crossed.

"Don't ever finish building your dream house," she said, barely reading the listing agreement. "Look what happened to me."

"Would you like to study the terms and call me back tomorrow night?"

"No. I'm ready to sign," she said, scribbling her name away.

It is cool these September mornings. Except for an elderly man and his dog, I am the only one out. The first day I ran on the beach I worried about the dog, a thick-necked German shepherd standing in my path. But the dog had tired of the chase and stood by his master's side, nonplussed. The man lifted his head as I passed, said "morning," and stooped lower to search for objects that others had left behind or forgotten. I huffed "lovely out," and headed for the rocky cliff at the far end.

In the spring of the third year of my married life, Jim suggested we take a day off and go somewhere.

"Yes, let's," I said, passing him in the kitchen door on the way to a brokers' opening.

The next day he made club sandwiches and wrapped them twice to keep them fresh. He packed six cans of beer, toothpicks, silver forks and knives, and lemon juice to clean our sticky hands. He brought a transistor TV to watch his game. "Baseball is about life. It's full of nuance and gesture," he told me. "You should try to appreciate it, Laura."

But I hated sports and didn't even try.

Funny how I run every day now.

JIM DROVE TWENTY miles north of Boston to a seaside resort. We stopped at a park near the water. He watched TV. I looked at seagulls picking through trash.

"Jim, I'd like to walk around."

"Sure, after this inning."

"I thought we were spending the day together?"

"We are. Shh, oh my sweet Moses, he did it!"

"How much longer?" I started to gather our things. Anyway, the late April sky had clouded over and I could smell the ionized air. Two seagulls circled above.

"It might rain," I said.

"It won't rain." He snapped off the TV and stood up. "See? Game's over. Ready?"

We walked in and out of gift shops. We nodded our way through several art galleries, looked at etchings marked down half price, passed a caricature painter on the sidewalk. At the end of the street, I spotted a tiny shop called "Three Stars" hidden in an alleyway. The crescent shaped sign shifted like a weathervane in the light breeze.

"How quaint," I said, pointing to the sign. I hurried toward it.

The bookshop smelled of fresh pine. I didn't see any cardboard witches on display. A plump woman draped in an afghan sat behind the counter, reading. Her light hair had been smoothed into a bun, smooth as her skin.

"Can I help you with something?" she asked, unwrapping herself.

Jim made a face and went over to the Philosophy section.

"Yes, what are those?" I pointed to the glass case next to the register.

"Which one? The amethyst? The citrine?"

"Come on, Laura," Jim whispered into my neck. "Let's go."

"The purple one," I said. I bent down for a closer look.

The woman opened the glass case with a key and pulled out a purple rock the size of my fist.

"Amethyst. You have nice taste." She placed the rock in my hand.

"Come on," he whispered again and went over to the door. He stood with his hand on the knob. Disgust made the light in his dark eyes glitter then recede. I turned away.

"What music is playing?" I asked the woman and handed her back the rock. The harmonies filled my head like incense.

"Music of the seventh plane. We sell the tapes. They're very popular."

The door banged shut and Jim was gone. In his absence I walked over to the section on "ROCKS" and pulled out a book on precious stones. I read about diamonds and citrines. Each stone had its own temperament, color and hue. I bought the book, thanked the woman for her help, and left.

I stood on the curb and looked around for Jim. At the opposite end of the street I watched a man and woman stop in front of a bakery shop, then go inside. It had grown cool and grey. A paper bag flew against my legs. I hugged my arms. Still, no Jim. I headed back to the car.

On the main avenue, others hurried past me. People whispered as if the approaching storm might hear them and follow them home. I heard a child shriek.

The car was just as we had left it, empty and clean except for the picnic basket. Jim had the keys. All around me car doors slammed, muffled, wind-rushed sounds. I held my breath against the surrounding exhaust.

"Laura!" Jim yelled fifteen yards off. He came toward me waving a small box in the air. "You've got to try this cake." He opened the box and showed me a cleanly frosted white cake.

"Would you open the door?" I said. "It's cold and you have the keys."

"What's your problem?"

"Where were you? Where did you go?"

"You left," he said. "I went to the bakery, then I went back to the store but you weren't there. What's the big deal?"

A fat raindrop hit the frosting on his cake.

"I'm cold. Would you open the car, please?"

"You didn't wait long," he said. He tossed the box at me so that I barely caught it. "That woman looked like a witch," he added. "I see you bought something from her."

I got in. "It's just a book. She was very nice."

"Scammers always are," he said too quickly. "That's how they draw you in. Then they take your money. Try the cake."

When we turned onto the highway, raindrops splattered across the windshield. I bit into the cake and thought: so this is love.

"What do you see in that New Age stuff?" he began again. "It's for loony people. It's voodoo. You should know that. If you're looking for answers, why don't you go to church like normal people do? You're an intelligent woman. I'll go with you if you want."

"Turn the headlights on," I said. "Besides, you don't want to know."

"What are you, an old wise woman?" he asked, accelerating. "A Sage-ess?"

"Miserable," I said for the very first time.

When we got home, he watched the sports roundup. I went upstairs and hid the book in my sweater drawer. A steady rain was no time to drive people around, so I called the office for messages.

Every day the sweat breaks into a misty web across my breasts. Every day I cross this space, cross this sand, this problem between Jim and me. But the problem shifts without sound underneath, eludes me like the driftwood I see slowly twisting its way along the shoreline.

• • •

DURING THE WINTER of the fourth year of my marriage, my old college friend, David, invited us over to meet his new wife. He met Lydia in his research lab. They both worked together on the mutation of cells. The wedding had been small; things happened too quickly to plan something big, Dave told me over the phone. "Four ecstatic months," he explained. "Wait until you meet Lydia."

"Well, well," I laughed. "Glad to hear you're in love."

The dinner party was in February, a night so cold the stars shriveled up like spiders in the sky. Thin ice caused me to slip on the steps to David's house. I grabbed the railing just in time. Jim had already gone ahead to ring the bell.

"Hello strangers!" David said when he opened the door.

Lydia had delicate wrists and arms. She held out her hand and looked into my eyes when she said hello. I shook hands with Raymond and met Raymond's date, a vogue-simulation of a woman named Suzanne. I disliked her from the start.

Suzanne had legs longer than a back door shadow, blond white hair, a leather skirt that pinched her hips and waist. She wore pinecone earrings. Raymond, on the other hand, wore a flannel shirt torn in the shoulder seam. I had a feeling he would look good in anything. Jim wore a dark suit and tie, impeccably tailored. As for me, I wore a simple, red silk dress.

David showed us into the living room where chemistry books filled every bookcase. My realtor's eye instinctively rearranged the cluttered room. The breakfront should have been up against another wall. The wing chair and love seat needed recovering.

Jim strode over to an old-fashioned record player. "You ought to get yourself one with a laser instead of a needle, Dave," he said. "They work great."

"Love to," David answered. "With the few extra bucks I don't have. How about a drink everyone?"

Lydia came around with the cheese tray. Her earrings glistened when she moved. David bent over and kissed the back of her neck.

"Bravo! Bravo!" Suzanne clapped in my ear.

Bravo what? I turned away from her and looked over at Raymond sitting by himself on the love seat.

He smiled. I smiled back. In the middle of the room Jim busily unscrewed the champagne cork. "Cheers!" he cried when it popped.

"Ray's looking for a house," David said, handing me a glass. "Did he already mention it?"

"Not yet," Raymond said, coming over.

"Good. You can talk about it over dinner. Everyone!" David announced. "Take your seats! Couples split up. I want you all to get acquainted."

I walked with Raymond into the dining room.

"What are you looking for?" I asked.

"A wife."

"Excuse me?" I said.

"Anything's possible." Suzanne said. She readjusted her skirt and sat down next to Jim.

"She's a beauty," Raymond whispered to me, "But she's not for me. How about a date this evening?"

I laughed and pulled out a chair. Raymond sat down beside me. The honeymooners took their positions at the head and foot of the table. By then, Suzanne had already unhooked one of her cones and was handing it to Jim.

"I hear you're a real pro at work," Raymond began. "Or do you deny it?"

"I let people judge for themselves."

"I always do. How long have you been married?"

"Four years. How long have you been single?"

"Four years," he said. "Same as you. I was married once." He looked at me with crystal blue eyes, so clear they stunned me. Then he turned and raised his voice.

"I'd like to make a toast." He stood and waited for everyone to quiet down, then began to speak in the cadence of Shakespeare. "Let me not to the marriage – " he began, looking first at Dave and Lydia. The word marriage sent me down a silent tunnel until I heard "'Time's fool,'" and I exited. Raymond finished and sat down.

Both David and Jim clapped for more.

"Thanks," Raymond said. "But it's the only one I know by heart."

"How did you learn to recite like that?" I asked.

"I'm a man of many selves. Stockbroker, occasional actor, occasional fool," he nodded, laughing.

"Fool?"

"In love."

"A fool in love like the rest of us," I mumbled before taking a long sip of my drink. I'd been busy writing contracts, returning phone calls. What did I know about love? All day I talked about slopes in the floor, cracks in the kitchen wall, leaks, divorces.

"Glasses!" Jim announced. "Here's to love and a long marriage, *communication*," he said with emphasis, "And a great sex life!"

Everyone laughed.

I smiled.

Raymond nodded.

David carved the leg of lamb while everyone helped themselves to beans and potatoes and salad. Jim talked to Suzanne and Lydia. David interrupted Jim. Raymond and I talked to each other, mostly about work.

"One of my clients disconnected his phone," I explained, putting my fork down. "He put his house on the market then changed his mind. But he was afraid to tell me. I called and wrote. Finally, I drove to his house at seven in the morning and surprised him. We worked it out. He just called me the other day. He's thinking of selling again."

"That's why you're successful. You don't give up."

I shrugged. "That's business. Tell me about acting. What's the most important thing?"

"Credibility, of course, though I'm no pro. You have to connect with just one person out there in the audience. Like you," he said suddenly. "You need to connect – "

"How would you know?"

"Sixth sense."

That unnerved me and I turned to Jim watching Suzanne making a point with her red polished nails. Both earrings were on the tablecloth beside his plate. I was about to excuse myself to go to the ladies room, when the doorbell rang.

"I asked some friends for dessert," David said, getting up to answer the door. Several couples piled into the hallway creating a squall of laughter.

"Wife," Jim said to me, his voice loud from champagne and wine. "I want to dance. Let's start the music."

"Jim, later. Not now."

"Come on, Laura. Dance. Come on."

He came around and pulled me into the living room, toward the stack of records.

"I'm not in the mood right now."

"You're never in the mood," he said, walking away.

I went upstairs to the bathroom and sat on the rim of the bathtub. The doorbell rang several more times. More laughter. Someone put on a Beatles' album. I whispered the phrases I knew from the songs and traced a moldy line of caulking between the floor tiles.

"Where did you disappear to?" Raymond asked when I reached the bottom of the stairs. "You're my date, remember?"

"I'm sorry," I said.

We walked back to the living room. Several couples were dancing. Other couples passed between rooms carrying plates of brownies and ice cream, nodding hello. More people arrived. In the middle of all this, Jim danced with Suzanne. Her arms hung all over his shoulders.

"I think, actually, we may leave soon," I said.

"One dance," Raymond said. "It'll boost my self-esteem."

Always, after I finish running, I mount the steps to my cottage two at a time, snapping past the grasses that are tough and poke at my skin.

RAYMOND'S SHIRT WAS soft against my chest the night we danced. He pressed his hand to my back and we moved in a small arc, not turning. I smelled the shampoo in his hair and for a moment, I closed my eyes. Then the music changed to something fast again. Jim came over and said it was getting late.

"It was a pleasure to dance with your wife," Raymond said. "Maybe she'll show me some houses sometime. I'll call you about it," he said, looking at me.

Jim clamped his arm around my waist, pulling me in.

The man and his dog are already gone at the end of

my run and I start thinking that the problem isn't just a problem but a matter of fate, like that man and his dog. Fate runs if you run, walks if you walk. No matter what, it stays by your side.

That night after David's party, Jim swerved the steering wheel back and forth, his idea of a joke, his idea of everything under control. The car skidded across the snow and landed completely turned around in someone's driveway.

"Jim, Christ!" I said. "What are you doing?" The purple white light from the street lamp made our skin look stiff as shopping bags.

"You're drunk," I said. "Let me drive."

He put the car in reverse. I opened the door and planted one foot in the air. "I'm getting out."

"Don't get hysterical, Laura."

"I'm getting in the back seat."

"Go ahead. You do what you want anyway. You had such a good time with your new friend; next time I'll stay home."

"I see. Is that what's going on here? You certainly had a good time with your new friend," I said.

"Get in, Jesus," he said looking into the rear view mirror at an approaching car. He yanked on my coat and reached across my lap to shut the door. "Don't make a scene. This could be their driveway."

"You're the scene," I laughed bitterly.

During these six weeks of living alone, I have twice walked into the kitchen and started stripping everything off. I imagine myself on film, the camera following me around my three small rooms. After I've unhooked my bra, the camera closes in on a shot of my clothes on the kitchen floor. Next thing, I'm in the shower. The window is open

*and the air is mixed with the smell of soap and the sea. I
dress, put on make-up and walk out to the parking lot to
a cheering crowd.*

"Who's unhappy today?" I ask the receptionist, a small-
breasted college student who works part-time at the realty
office. I usually stop at her desk when I come in.

"Mr. Raymond Martell. He's called twice."

I collect my pink slips and walk down the aisle of
cubicles. Mine's at the end. On the way, I'll stop to chat
with the others unless it's the lunch hour. That's when all
the realtors are out. For a few weeks, Jim called almost
every day around twelve-thirty.

"How are you feeling today?" he asked.

"The same. You?"

"When are you coming home?"

"I don't know."

Raymond is dark like Jim, but shorter. The night
we danced our ears touched. For months I remembered,
until the picture of him was so deep down in my mind I
couldn't see it anymore; until he reappeared one morning
knocking on my cottage door, emerging out of the dark
like a diver coming up for air.

"Remember me?" he said through the screen.

"Yes. Of course. Do you always get up this early?"

"When I want to see you. How about a walk?"

I hesitated. A bird fluttered behind him.

"I've been feeding them," I explained, opening the
door. "Now they expect to be fed." I closed the door
and got a loaf of bread from the refrigerator. "Take
some. " I opened the door again, handed him the loaf
but stayed inside.

"I left two messages," Raymond said, persisting. "Did
you ever get them?"

"Yes. I did. I'm sorry I never called you back."

Several more birds surrounded Raymond's feet.

"That's enough!" I shouted. The birds started fighting for the crumbs. I opened the door again and waved them away. "Sea pigeons. That's what they really are." My bathrobe was flannel but I crossed my arms, afraid he could see through it.

"Would you wait here a moment?" I said, disappearing into the bedroom. I grabbed a blouse and shorts and dressed frantically in the bluish morning light.

"This is crazy," I said, joining him outside.

"Fools are crazy, remember?" he said, smiling at me.

"Maybe they are, maybe not."

We stopped on the steps to watch the sun burning up the sea.

"I'm still looking for a house," he said.

"How do I know you're serious?"

"I fell in love at a party." He turned away and started down the stairs. "That's serious enough."

I followed him down, amazed. He wore a short-sleeved shirt, his sturdy arm muscles so unlike Jim's wiry, runner's arms. We crossed the sand and walked alongside the water.

"Close your eyes," he said. "I'm going in."

Icy smooth waves gleamed and cracked.

"I have to watch this," I said.

He unzipped his pants but kept his underwear on, then tossed his shirt and dungarees on the ground.

"Here's to something good," he added and dove in.

I caught a glimpse of his firm, round butt in spite of myself and laughed when he sauntered out dripping. Jim would have gone back to get the bathing suit, the towel, the latest style in slippers before going in. I laughed again.

"You can use my shower," I offered.

"'A women's beauty,'" he recited, grinning, "'Is like a white/Frail bird ... '" He was cheerful, waving his arms in the air. Then he stopped. "You feeling happier these days?" He rolled up his clothes and tucked them under one arm.

"I don't know about happy."

"I was talking to Dave about you," he said, touching my cheek.

I looked down at the hairs on his legs, smoother than a seal's.

"You don't love Jim. I knew that evening at Dave's."

"That's my business."

"Nobody else's."

I started walking away toward the stairs.

"Where you running to?" he called after me.

"Listen. I'm sorry," I said, stopping. I feathered the sand with my toe. "Would you like some coffee?"

At the house, Raymond showered quickly, drank a cup and went home. When he left I sat absorbing the new air in my house, as if it had blown up from the dunes. My mind felt lighter, full of jet streams. The phone rang once but I let the machine take care of it. Finally, I got up to take a shower only to discover his underwear in a clump under the pedestal sink. It startled me; soft white jockey shorts on the hard white ceramic tile. I left them there. Should I have thrown them in the wastebasket? One way or another, it wouldn't have mattered in the end.

More days passed, ten eleven hours when my mind undulated upward and back. I got home from driving around, turned on the machine, stared at my hands, waited for some kind of answer to wash ashore, some kind of relief.

But only work thoughts like invisible organisms filtered in:
how I needed to call a bank, or a house inspector or the
surveyor of someone's land, and once again I began listen-
ing to messages, rewinding the tape, returning calls, set-
ting up appointments, convincing Mr. And Mrs. X why a
certain house was perfect for them, well-priced, why they
shouldn't wait.

"I'M LOOKING FOR a house; can you help me?" Raymond
asked. It was his opening line three weeks ago when he
walked into my office for the very first time.

"Possibly," I said.

I showed him an old Victorian not far from Saltwater
Pond, just outside the city. An elderly man lived there
for thirty-six years.

"'Call out dear secrets!'" Raymond shouted to the
empty walls. Not a single chair had been left behind.
He started up the stairs. I followed.

"It's got four bedrooms," I explained. "Three on the
second, one on the third floor. What do you think so far?"

"I think there's plenty of room for you and me, and
guests, if we feel like it."

"Fantasy life," I said.

"Bet you have one, too."

He inspected the bathroom, the medicine chest, the
drawers in the linen cabinet. He turned on the faucet
and we watched the water drain slowly.

"I don't know," he said. "This plumbing could
dampen my fantasy."

"It'll cost you. The master bedroom's to the left."

I walked down the hall. The floors creaked and my
heels clattered against the floorboards. Raymond wore

sneakers. He disappeared into the master closet, suddenly, soundlessly. I opened the window in the bedroom and saw an old discarded pillow lying under a tree.

"Let's go downstairs," I called to him.

He reappeared and followed me down. "Are you going to go back to him, Laura?"

I gripped the banister. "How can you ask?"

"You ought to make up your mind."

"Why?"

"So I can make love to you."

"Oh, God," I said, sitting on the step.

He looked at me and his eyes asked me to open up.

"I can't yet," I said gently.

He nodded. "Listen," he said, sitting beside me. "Dave told me you were a lot happier in college."

"Everybody was."

"That's cynical."

"How do you know David?" I asked.

"We grew up together. Same neighborhood. Same schools."

I looked through the balustrade at the empty hallway below. Several keys were available. I knew any realtor could walk in.

"We'd better go," I said.

I dropped him off at his car in front of my office and went back to my desk to check messages. The man who had been afraid to put his house up for sale called me back once again.

"Laura," he began when I answered. "You won't believe this, but I'm not ready to sell. I don't mean to sound crazy," he added, coughing into the phone, "but damn, it just doesn't feel right."

"Go with your feelings. You don't want to force it. Call me when you're ready." I wished him well and hung up.

That same day I went back to the Three Stars bookstore.

"They stimulate consciousness," the woman said, boxing up the crystal. "Make sure it gets plenty of light."

When I returned to the cottage I put the quartz rock on the windowsill next to the bed. Jim would have thought it was foolish. "Where's your brain, Laura?" he would have said. Maybe most people would have thought so too. A crystal is like a heart. If you look into it long enough you'll see the essence, your emotions pared down to clear matter.

A few days later I called Jim.

"We need to talk."

"You mean you're ready to end your vacation from me?"

"It's not a vacation."

"Okay. Stay there. I'll be over."

I sat on the front step of the cottage, no longer waiting. He came just before dark, carrying sandwiches and a six-pack of beer, looking thinner, more determinedly himself. He sat next to me, his long legs stretched out.

"Okay, Laura, what's the problem?"

I began slowly. "We don't see things the same way. Do we? I mean. Maybe we haven't for a long time. Maybe we never did. I'm not trying to find fault."

He nodded to himself. "I'll tell you what I've been thinking. I think you want a baby. It's time. I think you've really blown this out of proportion. We've both been busy."

I bit into the sandwich but I didn't want it.

"You know," he said, finishing his beer. "You're always upset. I think you should see a therapist."

"What's therapy got to do with this?" I asked, standing.

"All you think about is Laura. It's pathetic."

"I'm pathetic then," I said.

He stood up and went inside to go to the bathroom. I watched a whirl of bugs bang stupidly against the kitchen light.

"You goddamn bitch!" he said, kicking open the door.

I flinched. "What? What!"

"Collecting men's underwear? Didn't take you long."

"That's not true!" I said, reaching my hand out. "Jim wait! Jim!" I screamed.

He started to sprint and quickly turned the corner out of sight. I went inside and started scrubbing the coffee stains on the stove. I scrubbed the sink. I washed the floor. I kept looking at the clock. The hands hardly moved. When I was certain he would be home, I pushed the automatic dial on the phone. No answer. I pushed it again. The continuous ringing numbed my ear. He had to be home. I slammed down the receiver and ran to the car.

When I arrived at my old house, every room was lit up, none of the shades drawn, except one. For a moment I sat in the car but I guess no dog or master of fate needed to tell me what to do. I rang the doorbell. No response, except the sound of the CD's bass vibrating through the door. I went around to the basement and let myself in.

In the dark I smelled our laundry soap and the clean linoleum tiles. I started up the basement stairs. He opened the door.

"What do you want," he asked, looking down at me. He stood at the top, a glass in his hand.

"I want to explain."

"Get out – "

"Jim, it's not what you think."

He slammed the door. I heard him running toward the front of the house.

I went out again to the end of the driveway and saw him in my car, a darkness in the dark behind the wheel.

"Jim – ." I got in the passenger side.

"I'm driving you home, Laura."

"This is my car. Will you let me explain?"

"Explain what? You can have a fucking divorce. I don't have *time* for this shit. I want a normal life."

"Jim. This friend came over," I said. "We took a walk. He went swimming. I let him take a shower."

"Shut up, just shut up!" he shouted, pounding his fist on the dashboard. "Who are you kidding, Laura?" He went for the keys in the ignition but I was quicker and pulled them into my lap.

"This can't work can it?" I whispered.

"No, it can't." He rested his forehead against the rim of the steering wheel. "You know why? You enjoy conflict. You need it. You *love* it."

A neighbor's spotlight lit up the car like police. "Let's not start again."

"I need to lie down," he said, squinting. "They're bright and I'm tired. I'm going in."

"Please. I'll come in with you."

We followed the pied piper of habit, up the familiar front walk to the house and beyond, into the mountainside. On the way upstairs, he put his arm around me. By the top of the second floor landing he had my sweater off and was fumbling with my bra. I didn't stop him. I switched off the guest bedroom light, the study light, and in our bedroom, the two night table lamps that had both been turned on as well. I leaned back on the bed so he could ease off my pants. Then I pulled him down.

I pulled on his hips and listened to our bedroom shade flapping in the wind, sucking our past out with the breeze. We pushed and pulled but we never found the insides. He turned over into a dark hugging sleep. I rolled off the bed and slipped away for the very last time.

For the remainder of that night, I stayed on the single bed kneeling at the cottage window, my nose pressed against the soft screen mesh gasping, holding my breath, the sky so endlessly black I could have drowned in it, except for the moon, tiny bright hole in the sky, and the memory of Raymond and Jim distantly shining, breaking through.

For at that time in my life, I am sorry to say, I was too brittle and hollow for any man's reach.

A relic of my future.

A shell.

Bird of Grief

I woke to the beating between my legs. No sleeping in that state. Every day, darkness seeped back into the light and, of course, my dreams suffered. Three months post-Richard I lay curled around the slow alarm song of my cell phone: a dark indentation on my pillow next to my ear.

Finally, I got up and went to where this boy, who was not Richard, might be. I walked along University Avenue, the long stretch of sidewalk decreasing as I neared the college quadrangle. My fingers curled nervously in my coat pocket as he approached, returning from class. So many times we ran into each other like this. I told myself it was more than coincidence

The first time I stopped him, I said, "Excuse me. What is your name?" This took him by surprise. He cleared his throat, his lips moist as the earth in that November drizzle. I wondered if they were as cold.

"Seth, and yours?

"I'm Jennie." Then, rushing: "Where did you grow up? Where are you from?" I sipped my breath, warping an ant's worth of pocket lint between my fingers.

"A farm out West, but not a real farm," he said. "We had land near the hills."

"I'm from the city. Much different than you, I imagine."

"I would think so."

I touched his arm and went away to my filmmaking class. I was late, though a few steps later I turned to watch him receding in the weather. Drops of what I didn't know about him filled my brain. He wasn't Richard but maybe he could be.

Seth wore dark corduroy pants, wire-rimmed glasses, neatly cropped hair, a blazer. I guess I was impressed. I wore red pants, a green plaid scarf that mismatched. My savage blond curls rejected most types of barrettes. I didn't think it mattered once you turned off the light.

In my daydreams I found him alone in an empty schoolroom. He was expecting me. I slipped a hand under his chin; unzipped his pants. My hand searched beneath his cotton shirt, past daylight into the dark humming in his chest, until our bodies were pieces of cloth we had left behind, our invisible selves afloat someplace away from earth. It was all I could muster: to fly free across a current of clouds, until we drifted back into the light, that simple classroom.

I dreamt this again and again but it still wasn't enough to take me away from Richard, who blended in with those winter birch trees that first time we met skiing in Vermont two years ago. Even in ski gear he looked sinewy, beautifully self-contained. Paired up on the double lift by coincidence, we sat together talking. Richard told me he studied math.

"Here's a puzzle," he said. "There's a boat in the ocean at low tide. Hanging from the boat is a rope ladder with six rungs." He pointed his skis down at the people shushing below, colorful pompoms dancing on their heads. "The water comes up to the first rung. Are you with me so far?"

"Keep going."

"Where does the water come to at high tide?"

I pictured a boat anchored at sea. Did the ladder go down? Did the rungs disappear?

"I don't know. Just tell me."

"First rung. Know why?" He eased into his professorial mode. "Because the boat floats." He looked at me then with clarity in his face. Simple. "Math is universal. But people fear it. It's all about looking at the same thing in many different ways. That's the beauty of it."

The beauty of him, I thought.

"Tell me another riddle." By then, I was sitting up in his hotel bed, pulling off my thermal shirt. We wrapped ourselves in his goose down sleeping bag. Two years later on the phone, Richard said he felt claustrophobic. With five states separating us, a fourteen-hour bus ride, twelve hours in my car if I drove from Rhode Island to North Carolina on the highway late at night, the time apart didn't add up, he said. He came to Providence five maybe six times during the middle period. Then he stopped.

"What do you mean claustrophobic? What's not adding up?"

"People change," he said over the phone.

So I found Seth on the campus quadrangle. He was looking at me, too. Neither one of us said much except for the questions in our eyes, the fringe of his woolen scarf fingering the breeze, not me, just inches away. His voice resembled the dusk I would have preferred; soft and dim, it made me want to forget conversation, get in and drive to that place-between-his-legs, then rest in the quiet way he walked beside me as we headed to the convenience store.

That morning was steeped in winter glare.

"Weren't you in my film class?" I was certain I saw him sitting near the door.

"Sort of. I dropped it. Can you wait? This will only take a minute." He squashed his dying cigarette with his snow boot. He didn't apologize for smoking.

Inside the store, I couldn't see well in the pharmaceutical light except for the region in his eyes that said he wanted me too. Or maybe he wanted to wait. He bought two crisp new packs while I fumbled around the shelves of notebooks, touching the ones with covers burning red.

Another week passed before I asked Seth to dinner. It had already snowed twice. I told him I needed to make a short clip for my final exam. Would he be my target subject? He accepted, offering to pick me up at the triple-decker where I rented a room on the top floor.

First, the buzzer, my voice calling to him as I leaned over the railing. "Do you want to come up for a minute?" I looked down at him through the stairwell's spiraling tunnel.

"Can't. Motor's running. I'll wait for you in the car." He tilted his head up and looked as if he were in a hole.

His red Volkswagen Bug bloomed like a flower in the cold. An impossible, beautiful sight. I got in, smiled hello. He shifted gears and drove. In another week it would be Christmas. Vacation time. He said he wasn't going home. "Family misunderstandings," he explained.

"What kind of misunderstanding?"

"It's nothing."

"Tell me."

"My parents are divorced. My father doesn't talk. He spends his life in the garage fixing radios."

"No, that doesn't sound good at all."

"Don't tell me you have ideal parents," he said.

I tilted my head; half smiled. "They were toxic. My father died in a violent crash."

He looked at me differently after that. People usually do. A combination of compassion spliced with envy as if being close to tragedy gave me an edge on living.

"My mother remarried when I was thirteen," he told me after that. "My father is bitter."

I wore a purple sweater under my aqua down coat and nestled in the seat, the squashed up place where New Orleans jazz played gaily on his CD, louder than the heat blowers sirening through the vents. He shifted gears again. We were off to a restaurant downtown, in the Italian section of Providence.

In this historic city we followed badly paved streets, buildings where people used to live. But he knew his way. He turned down an alley, rubbed one wheel against the curb to park. I got out and stretched my leg across an ice puddle, winging my arms out for balance.

"Did your parents fight a lot?" I walked beside him now on the sidewalk. "Or did they stop talking?" When my wrist nicked him accidentally and electrified, I grabbed my other mitten to ground myself.

"One way or another, it wasn't love. There," he said, pointing away from me toward the restaurant. "That's it."

At dinner, I layered our table with yellow pads of paper and file cards.

"Why pick me?" he asked. "You have friends."

"I wanted someone I didn't know."

"You won't discover much. You'll have to make things up. Lie a lot."

"Tell the truth," I said.

We sat in a room with red paper tablecloths, green window shades. When the meal came, I wound spaghetti strands around my fork. The noodles fell apart and I tried again. He thought it was funny.

"Don't look at me while I eat then," I said, squirming.

"You're looking at me. I'm looking at you. Why don't you tell me why you really want to make this film?" He stabbed the fleshy curl of a shrimp and slipped it neatly between his lips.

I dropped my fork, triggered to defend myself.

"You figure it out."

"I think I have." He eyed my plate.

"Think of it as a game. Start anywhere," I said tearing the cellophane wrap and pulling out a file card. I wrote: SCENE 1. Crummy Italian marching music ekes out of speaker in ceiling.

"What do you want to know?"

"Whatever you want to tell me."

Lights flickered in the underground room. The brick floor and walls seemed to make him crouch closer. He told me a story about his first days at the University, how he had left a suit jacket and pants in the train station locker, how they were stolen, and then, how he went there still thinking he could get them back.

"It's a lost cause," I said, which I regretted because he frowned.

He shrugged.

"Sorry. I didn't mean that. Tell me more about your parents. What happened between them?"

"Nothing happened."

"Aren't you upset about it?"

"Not anymore. It's old."

"Really? I don't believe you. Life's sad." As soon as I said that, I fell inside the hole that Richard left, my skin burning like snowballs stuck to my palms.

IF A TREE doubled in size every day for one hundred days, on what day would it become half its size? Richard asked me this a few days before the end. He was living with two math students off campus. His apartment was in a house. A dentist worked on the first floor. In the morning, at exactly nine o'clock, the drilling began. The odor of metal and toothpaste followed. Richard baked bread to erase the smell of it. In the refrigerator, he coddled mixtures of Russian black bread and sour rye dough in soda glasses.

I considered the tree puzzle. I didn't know the answer right away, as Richard would; then it came to me like Venetian blinds opening.

"The day before," I answered.

"Correct. Time for quantum mechanics class." He looked over my head at the kitchen clock. "You coming?" He stood at his front door.

"People can be that way too," I said, caught up in the possibilities of many meanings. "You know. Half of who they were the day before."

"That's not the same as the tree. The tree got bigger," he said, impatiently.

THE DAY AFTER dinner with Seth, I took my camera and went to the train station, a cavernous building, to search for his missing clothes or so I thought. The light was bad inside but I shot things anyway, running the lens along a wall of metal lockers, stopping at one with a heart scratched into it – a marred heart etched into the shape of a triangle. Pen lines crossed at each curve. The metal door was rusted and wouldn't budge like Richard. I capped the lens and went back to my apartment.

The next day Seth caught me wearing yellow tinted ski goggles.

"What are you doing? The sun's not out."

I turned full circle. "They brighten everything," I said. "Try them." I dangled the pair in front of him.

"You're crazy." He stood there for a moment, wondering.

"It's for my project."

I didn't tell him about the red-tinted glasses or the blue ones both in my book bag. I didn't tell him how the blue glasses didn't change much except to darken the air. Yet, blue was so familiar: blue sky, blue sea. Yellow took its claim from the sun. But those red glasses made me feel I could breathe underwater. I felt different, part of something unearthly; like that first time on the ski slopes with Richard when he stayed with me, sliding his skis alongside mine as we waited for the chair lift to take us up the mountain again.

Richard said he wanted to eat my thighs. That was in North Carolina. Middle period, first year. During that fall season down south he wore black jeans, hiking boots; his ski jacket heedlessly unzipped.

At home I walked around my bedroom wearing red goggles, staring, then pausing to stand over the bed. Red made the quilt ripple below me in a watery atmosphere. I imagined Richard floating on his back waiting for me to perch. I lay down on the mattress.

• • •

ONCE, TO MY surprise, I called out to Seth across the street: "Hey!" Another time, I called him "Sullen One" instead of saying hello. *Sexy*, I said to myself over and over and over to stay calm.

Then it grew hectic the way it always did before long school vacations: everyone packing, arranging train schedules, air travel. Not me. I walked out of the film room, down the old wooden stairs to the sidewalk to meet him.

Seth said, "Let me film you today."

"What? No. That's not my plan."

"Let me shoot you. That will tell you something about me."

"Hell it will." But I handed over my camera anyway, and tromped off to a large beech tree across the road. When I stopped and faced him again I stood blinking, twirling my eyes, covering my face.

"Don't do that," he shouted. "Take your hands away."

I laughed. "I'll do what I want!"

We walked to the coffee shop on the hill. I went inside and ordered two large, cream-no-sugars to go. Later, in the editing room, I watched my face brighten and dim behind the neon-lit glass of the restaurant. I saw myself talking to a waitress with gray hair, my hands wrapped around Styrofoam white cups. Small hands that he kept shooting. Couldn't keep his eyes away.

"What are you pointing at?" I asked, coming out of the restaurant. I looked down at the steps to avoid tripping. The lens hid his face – his knees bent, poised to move in.

"Random objects."

"I'm not random."

"Sure you are."

"Let me have that back." I reached for the camera. "No more filming me. The rest of today I shoot you. Get in your car."

He had a zealot's affection for his Bug: rusted spots, tears in the back seat, magazine covers rain-washed on the floor. I made him sit with the windows open. The wind blew his hair, his hands whitened with cold. I shot his half-face in the rear-view mirror. I shot his thighs, his crotch, the steering wheel, back to his hands on the wheel near his crotch. He had such delicate fingers.

"Close your eyes," I said.

"Why? What's this about? Where do I fit in?"

"I don't know yet. Keep your eyes closed until I tell you to open."

"So you can take me apart," he said, biting his lip.

"If you'll let me."

He nodded, one hand resting on the steering wheel.

"All right, you can get out now," I said.

I didn't see him again until Monday, three days before the University would empty out. He was busy over the weekend. Something about a friend. I spent the weekend thinking I should have been with him, pacing the streets, walking past his apartment – two days, blackened windows. Where was he?

I took my camera and roamed until Sunday night when, late, in my monstrous old sedan, I saw his shadow behind his window shade. Ten-thirty my fever waned. I tried to coast down the hill past where he lived and head home, but the traffic light turned red. My V-8 engine idled badly; loud enough I was certain an entire campus could hear. I swore at myself. Finally, the light turned green and I raced back to my room.

But Monday, yes. Once again, I got in his beloved car for a two-hour trip to Newport, though they said it might storm. The cold made my bones smart. I anchored the camera in my lap to stay calm.

"So. Did you go away?"

"Yep. With someone I shouldn't have been with."

"Really? That's never pleasant."

"Wrong. It often is."

"Oh," I said, somewhat shaken, because I thought of her: Richard's friend, roommate, new lover. She had spiky hair, Hawaiian eyes, a passion for math I couldn't muster.

As Seth headed for the seaside cliffs I promised myself that I did not want to know about this friend, did not want to know who she was. Then it began to snow. As soon as we turned onto the highway, it came down in flying slabs and skidded across the lanes. Traffic linked up and started sliding in bunches.

"Maybe we should turn back," I said.

"Okay, screw this." He pulled over to the side and waited with his hand on the stick.

"What is it? What's wrong?"

He looked perturbed as if his thoughts had turned into a ditch. He opened his coat and found a cigarette.

"How about if you film my apartment? Do you want to?" He looked at me.

"Yes, I would."

"It's not much."

"I don't care," I whispered. "Let's go."

He flicked the cigarette ash out the window and we got back on the highway: a few more miles, another exit onto a smaller road. The CD typed out burgeoning scales on the piano. Snowflakes clung to the rims of the window shield.

"See that turn there?" I said, pointing to his street.

"You know where I live," he said, turning.

We parked in a lot behind his building and climbed a short flight of stairs. I waited on the landing while he found the right key. I worried about the curls in my hair, my breasts, my perfume, the size of my ears, my teeth.

He touched the door and it drifted open. I hauled the camera inside, toward the radiator hissing at the far end.

"I'll make coffee," he said. "Or would you rather have wine?

"It's early. Coffee's good."

He switched on the lamp by the couch. The red shade tinged the wood floors, pale walls. I went over to the window and looked down through the snow at the traffic light that had caused me so much discomfort the night before. Now my chest found relief and I breathed.

A million white specks flung themselves at the glass when his arm moved in around my waist. I leaned back. His hair and clothes smelled of smoke and snow, his lips on my neck. I couldn't hear anything except for his hand touching my face, my ear, measuring my shoulder, my hip. The kettle moaned and startled us. We were partially undressed. "You still want it?" he whispered.

"Yes."

Desperately. I wanted to manage this.

"I'll be right back," he said.

In his bedroom I hurried under the blanket and cold sheets. Posters hung like wallpaper. Huge, fantastical faces. Black trumpeters thrust out of every empty space. Next to me, the white window shades dropped halfway to the sill. Below the sill, a bookcase was stuffed with used college texts, piles of Blues CDs, a photo album, a coconut shell and a hula doll from Hawaii.

"See, it's not much," he said, entering.

"Look at all your CDs." I took the cup and flicked the hot coffee with my tongue, testing it.

"I've loved Blues since I was twelve."

"Why twelve?"

He lay next to me on the bed and released the cup from my hand. "I guess I started noticing things."

I expected to know his body from my dream but didn't. Our clothes bunched together at the end of the bed. I lay my hands on his buttocks and pulled on the essence of what I had lost in Richard. Sand trucks thumped down roads somewhere in the distance, a muted sound. Inside me, Seth stiffened, then rested his head in the pillow.

We didn't say anything at first. I had an idea of what our lovemaking could have been like and wasn't. The memory of stretching beside Richard speared my chest.

"We're in our twenties," he explained. "You'll see it's really the best thing. I'm not ready to be needed so much."

"Listen to the snow," I finally said to Seth.

His cell rang then, like a ghost.

"Not now," he moaned. "Go away." His cell rang and rang.

"Pick it up," I said. "Please shut it off."

He answered.

"Yes. No," he said. "I can't." Then he listened. Then he said, "A friend." Then, "I will, later."

I fished for my underwear in the sheets and put them on.

"Where are you going?" he asked.

"I'm getting more coffee. Who was that?"

"A friend."

"Someone you're seeing?"

"No."

"Should I believe you?"

"Probably not."

I hooked my bra and snapped my legs into my pants, my arms into my shirt. Breaking my vow of not wanting to know, I asked: "Are you seeing anyone else, besides her?"

"Why?"

"Tell me."

"Sometimes." He leaned up against the pillow. I looked at his cell on the pillow, the room sealed as an igloo. Snowflakes dwindled outside. He pulled off the sheet to show me his penis had become small and drawn into itself. I retreated too, cold as ever with nothing to say: old hurt rooting deeper, seeking nourishment. I looked up, finally, at a mass of strangers in his eyes. So I left the room and went into the kitchen. There, on top of the refrigerator I saw the single stem rose, a bottle of wine one third full, as recently drunk as the weekend I imagined, and an empty candy dish.

He came into the kitchen, fully dressed. "You're upset," he said.

"I didn't say that."

"I would be." He slid the bottle into the cupboard.

"Speak for yourself then."

"Okay. Will you stay and have something to eat?"

"If you'll drive me home."

"What do you think I am?"

"I'm not sure."

"Give me some credit."

"I do."

"Look, the snow stopped," he said, changing the subject. He opened the refrigerator and pulled out a box of chocolates.

I wasn't hungry but I sat down and nibbled the sweets, rapidly improvising talk about other men I had been seeing. Small, silly lies. It was true that every day on the street I saw men – men who were taller or shorter than Richard, lighter or darker. Everything Richard.

If his love for me decreased by half every day for one hundred days, on what day would his love become half of what it once was?

Easy answer.

The last day.

"I really need to finish this film," I said, standing up. "I can use what I have. Thank you for your help." I snorted at the sound of my pseudo-formality, my need to pretend.

"I didn't do anything."

Then I said something about stillness after a storm, magnificent fresh air. He carried my camera to the car.

"I'll call you," he said when he dropped me off.

We kissed and I hurried up the stairs to my room, sterile and bright from the snow. Four inches had fallen. Ice patterns gleamed on my windows as if to say there was more to silence than I imagined. I took a hot shower to erase the cold, empty, tired, restless feeling inside. In the early afternoon, the quiet remained, so I slept.

I slept until evening, when he called.

"Can't see you tonight," he said. "How about tomorrow for lunch?"

"Who are you seeing tonight?"

"Why must you ask?"

"Why not?" I felt the sarcasm nipping my tongue.

"It's a question of tact."

"We'll see," I said, and we hung up.

He showed up the next day half-shaven, shirtsleeves unbuttoned. I swung my camera up from my hip and caught his eyes skittering across a low sky before we entered the college café. My stomach was sore from nerves. At the table I felt small as if he couldn't see me. I felt gigantic as if I were blocking his beautiful view. We sat amidst chattering, exam-free students, the feeling of bursting in the holiday air downtown. I ripped my napkin. And then it came: his bid to remain friends.

"Cliché – oh God, are you kidding me? I should laugh." I jiggled my ice water like a warning bell. Hurry up boy. Hurry up.

"No, I'm serious. You don't believe me."

"I do. It's just so plebeian, isn't it?" My wet glass circling made tiny infinity marks on the tabletop.

"I've upset you," he said. "You flattered me. I don't know what I want."

"Neither do I. You flatter yourself."

"You're angry."

"Indifferent."

He shook his head. "Come on, Jennie. Be honest."

Oh, yes. Honest. If I were honest, I would have said, "You're right. I'm heartbroken over Richard. I failed in love. I'm so desperate and lonely. I failed with you." But I needed more lies. I hadn't tired of the game. I told myself that I had won something by putting another man's flesh between Richard and myself.

HOME WAS AN interminable silence, sixteen blocks away. I counted, unable to unhinge my jaw to speak while he drove.

"Listen," he said as I was getting out of the car. "Don't cry over this."

"You egotist," I burst out as if I were yelling at Richard. "I'm not crying. Do I look as if I'm crying? You're uptight, you know? We slept together once. I didn't ask you to marry me."

"One thing leads to another. Whose idea was this?"

"Mine!" I said, and slammed the door.

He drove off.

I went straight to the editing room and spent more hours in the dark pushing buttons, rewinding, splicing his slender wrists folded over his thighs. Segments of him circled me like the steering wheel of his car, the rim of his eyeglass, a curved cheekbone angling away from me in the rearview mirror. I sank deeper into that room, drifting downward until I could drift no further down, and despite how I tried to hold on, waving my hands through the projector's barrel of light, those images broke apart on the screen, scattered naturally in a blizzard of wings, rippled back into muddy shallows.

Forgiveness

1

That restless summer I craved my only sister like hunger craves food, like fatigue craves sleep, like loneliness craves love.

2

That was the summer after our father died.

3

I took a temporary job transcribing medical reports. It was easy good money, mindless, all fingers and letters – my laptop balancing anywhere on tables in coffee shops, my bed, my studio apartment floor.

4

My life was missing air.

My older sister was coaching a women's wrestling team in Florida. That's odd, right? And she was living with a woman.

"She never hurts me," she said.

5

That summer I went to bars, waiting, running, chasing, tagging for guys. One guy took me for a ride in his convertible. After he dropped me off at home, I sat at my bedroom window, blouse ripped open, too flushed with sex to sleep.

One man down, how many more to go?

6

When we were kids, Ruth climbed the highest tree on our street, a crowded block lined with brick apartment buildings and two-family houses just outside of a Northeast city. While she was playing ball or hanging upside down on a limb, I was upstairs on my twin bed, grooming the plastic hair on my dolls. Father called me princess. He said Ruth should stop acting like a boy.

7

Our house was narrow and crowded; everything echoed off wooden stairs and floors. It didn't take much. Her homework not done, a misplaced comb sparked outrage and a hand slap across my sister's face. Ruth told him to shut up. More slaps. It didn't stop.

8

Each time, Mom whispered her desperate need to leave. She was pretty in a sad kind of way. Small shoulders, slumped; thin feet.

9

Each time he hit Ruth, I wanted to flee. Where would I go at age four, six, eight?

One night, Ruth came home late. I heard a car drive up, the car door click shut and his silence waiting for her on the front step. She didn't see him in the shadow. But

I saw his hand flashing up and down, up and down, her wet, red face gleaming in the streetlight.

"Screw you, Dad."

She ran for blocks.

Down the hall, Mother pretending sleep, and me?

The next day, father prostrated himself, groaning. He called Ruth over and over.

"Come home. Do you hear me?"

I lay on my side paralyzed, watching her empty twin bed. When Ruth returned, he bought her a spotted mutt from the pound. He built a doghouse and put it on our small front porch, gluing shingles to the roof, leaving open holes on the sides for windows.

You see, our father was nice, too.

My sister named the puppy Happy.

10

That summer after Dad died, I walked to the park near my apartment, a small green square between brick buildings. I watched sprinklers spinning, spitting waterblades whipping a net of spray over everything. Little rainbows flew up and twinkled in the daylight. I sat on the bench wondering if Ruth tired of gym sweat or the smell of mildew growing in terrycloth towels? Did the sound of metal lockers echo an empty feeling inside as it did for me?

11

I craved her like questions yearning for answers.

12

In the car, Mom had dozed off in the passenger seat. The monotonous dark rains turned greasy, the narrow road heading south onto a sleek surface that spun them into a guardrail. Dad, unbelted, smashed against glass. Mom survived broken ribs.

13

That summer I went to a hotel bar and met a man from Argentina. He didn't speak much English. My Spanish was worse. *Ola. Yo no hablo.* That was about it. We dove into bed, loveless drunks. After he conked out, I escaped into the cool summer night, crossing a street to catch a bus. I didn't see a car speeding toward me. The man at the wheel braked, skidded away, almost hitting me, his face scattering with barely missed disaster.

"Watch where you're going," he screamed.

I'm going to Florida, I thought after that. I need to see my sister.

14

Not long after she graduated from high school, Ruth moved to Florida, met a woman and stayed. That was seven years ago.

15

On the plane to Miami, I fell asleep next to a man in a plaid shirt and khaki pants. When I awoke, he passed me a glass of orange juice.

"I saved it for you," he said.

"I just dreamed I had twelve children," I told him, smiling, accepting the drink. "And I'm not even married."

"Well, you're young," he said. "I've got two blessings. A girl and a boy. Four and six. Take a look." He showed me two stamp-sized school pictures. "The boy is the oldest. Great kid. Obsessed with baseball. A real boy."

"What do you mean by real boy?" I looked closer at the photo.

"Well," he said, tilting his head as if he'd never considered this. "He's a good kid."

When we landed, the married man wished me good luck and we parted ways at the end of the exit ramp. I got into a cab.

16

In my hotel room ten floors overlooking Biscayne Bay, I washed my face. The bed was king-sized – so enormous – I lay on it and floated while two clouds crossed the picture window. Once, when Ruth's puppy hurt her paw from a nest of thorns, Dad carried her for a mile to the vet's, whistling the whole way to keep the puppy calm. But Happy died young from a rare immune disease.

17

The sun pressed against the hotel curtains. I unwrapped a glass at the mini-bar and poured my father's favorite drink – gin with a splash of water. I adjusted the thermostat and opened the closet door to explore. When I was little, I hid in our closet behind my sister's clothes and pretended I was a rich lady waiting for my train ride to start. Mother would come into my room and say: Jennie? Jennie? Where are you now?

That hotel room on Key Biscayne was my rich lady's suite. I walked all around, squished my toes into the rug.

18

Ruth owns a wood bungalow home on Marathon Key. The front porch slopes and one of the stairs is broken, the corner bitten off. Pink flowering Bougainvillea streams down one side.

"Ruth, hey! It's me," I called through the screen door, then opened it up and let myself in. She had a beige couch that sagged on one end. Laundry was piled on a dining room table. Sneakers in a pile next to the door.

"Jennie, What the hell?"

We hugged. She felt solid with good health: browned arms, her hair streaked with sun. Ruth is small. Her hands and ears shaped like mine.

As it turned out, she was leaving that night for a tournament in the north part of the state.

"My luck," I said. "I should have called."

"We might be champions this year."

"I'm not surprised." She had been winning blue ribbons since first grade.

"Do you need a place? Where are you staying?"

I told her about the hotel. In the kitchen, she poured two glasses of icy water.

"Come on. I'll take you out on the boat. I have time for that."

I followed her down a sandy path through tall grasses behind her house. She was so comfortable trudging through thorny leaves, but I thought those thick roots looked like snakes and they made me jumpy.

"It's okay, Jennie. Don't be afraid. They're just plants," she said, knowing me.

The trail ended on the beach, lined with Australian pines. They bowed over the sand like long feathers in a light wind. As I walked, the ocean emerged looking vast and chlorine green, almost fake. I had never seen such color. Her small motorboat was anchored in the shallow water. She held it steady as I climbed in.

"This heat," I said. I was burning up and pulled my skirt over my knees. The sun wrapped a thousand rays around my neck.

The boat rocked gently. I clasped the sides while Ruth pulled the string to start the motor. She yanked and the water blades roared.

"The one time you come to visit," she said.

"Not one time. I'm coming back. I'm glad I'm here now."

The waves glittered in the breeze. I watched six pelicans sweep inches above the water. She pointed to a fish jumping, then a sailboat in the distance. Clouds near the horizon changed color like distant waters. Slowly, individual trees on shore joined together into one, solid mass. She turned the motor off and we drifted.

"How have you been since Dad died," I asked.

"Pretty much the same. Mother seems to be doing fine."

"She's selling the house."

"Finally letting it go," Ruth said.

In her boat, she looked fragile and pretty in a way I'd never recognized. No anger marking her face.

"Don't you hate him?" The question blurted out of me like a cough. "How can you forgive him?"

"I don't hate him." She pulled the anchor line through her hands, looping it through her hands.

"I never helped you," I said. "I should have kicked him, screamed. Done something. I did nothing to protect you."

"You were too young, Jennie." She looked toward a tiny island far from our boat, far as the distance of six years between us. A flock of birds glimmered above that island. "He was a broken man, you know. A broken man. I tell myself this every day."

"It must have taken everything inside you to come to that," I said. "More than everything. More than everything," I said, repeating.

We didn't speak for a bit, allowing that truth to soak in. But time interrupted. She looked at her watch.

"Let me steer," I said, reaching for the tiller.

We switched places, carefully moving around each other, stepping over the middle seat. I pushed the tiller too hard at first, then discovered how minor adjustments of the tiller, an inch left or right, kept us on course.

"Easy," she said. "Works best."

I felt released from the shadow of violence and settled into that eternal moment of bright sun and sea: watching her relax, leaning back against a gently rising bow, her fingers skimming freely through salty waters.

Heart

The night before leaving for Paris to meet my lover, Raoul, I stood in the shower soaping away sweat, trying to calm myself. I was excited, nervous, a little scared. Neither one of us had been there. After my shower, my dog, Chili, hopped in circles catching her tail while I packed and paced inside my studio apartment, a converted garage behind my landlords' house in Miami. My air conditioner rumbled in the window, wrestling with Florida's maniacal September heat.

"Isn't it odd?" I said, calling Raoul one last time. It was midnight on my side of the world. He lived on the West Coast, in a one-bedroom apartment in the foothills of Los Angeles. We'd been splitting our bi-coastal commute all year. "None of the houses in Miami have basements." I plopped back on my bed.

"What's odd about it?"

"Think about it. This very second my bed is supported by a concrete floor, and underneath me is a meter of pure sand and underneath that a millennium-old layer of coral rock. Eons ago my bed would have been underwater." I stretched my bare legs and feet and looked up at the ceiling fan spinning above me. "I might have been a fish once, a long time ago."

"Likely,' he joked. "You sound like one. Go to bed. I'll see you in one more day."

"Will you recognize me?" I tilted my cell like an icy drink, sipping the sound of him.

"No."

"Tell me where you are?"

"In the kitchen, talking to you."

"Okay, goodnight. Dream about me."

"I always do."

"No you don't," I said, watching the white paddles of the ceiling fan. I tried to follow one paddle circling.

"I'm dreaming about you right now."

"Very funny. Goodnight."

I plugged my cell into its charger and tried to think about Raoul dreaming about me except the inside of his brain appeared dark as outer space, an underwater cave oblique and remote as the ancient ocean lapping at my cottage door. Shadows of his body floated over me like giant sea plants. I lay quietly, remembering the first time we met at a sales conference in L.A. We both sell software packages. He can sell anything because he knows how to smile. Raoul says one shake of my long, natural blond curls closes the deal.

I gave up following paddles in the air. My packed suitcase waited by the door. My landlords, Mimi, a pregnant lawyer, and her urologist husband, Jeff, kindly offered to watch my muzzle-faced angel while I was gone. Chili lay next to me on the cool floor. I leaned over to kiss her. A cricket started up in a pink flowering hibiscus bush outside my window. For a long time it sang by itself waiting for an answering call.

On the flight overseas, I took an aptitude test in a business journal to find out if I had success potential.

Do you have visions? one question asked.

Floor lights in the center aisle looked like iridescent bugs, so I checked *yes*, then tried dozing on the plane's bed of vibrations. The long night passed. I landed at dawn.

At the hotel address, I got out of the cab. A neon red sign said HOTEL LISZT at the far end of an unlit arcade, a tunnel lined with chintzy shops. I started toward it. A green arrow pointed the way. As I took tentative steps, glass storefronts flickered past me like an ominous aquarium, a closed-circuit museum where ancient animals once lived. Vendors' CLOSED signs hung lamely on strings. I reached the original, blood-colored carpet of the hotel. A tall but stern man stood behind a wood-paneled reception desk.

"I have a room, *une salle*," I said to him.

He raised his eyebrows when I mentioned Raoul's name.

"Monsieur Raoul is already upstairs. You may go ahead. Fourth level." He pointed to an elevator at the end of another dim hall.

WHEN THE ELEVATOR didn't respond to my call, I opted for the narrow, spiraling stairs. One level, two levels, turn; three levels, turn. It grew darker as I climbed upward, lugging my suitcase, my carry-on bag, too. Where were the lights in this grim, empty vault of a stairwell? Anxiety sucked away my breath. My suitcase felt heavier with each step. I tried imagining lovers spawning on the misty cliffs of Niagara Falls, but this darkness overwhelmed me. I felt a terrible foreboding. All I could see were crusty chips of ceiling plaster.

"Raoul! It's me." I knocked.

He opened the door and tried to kiss me.

"I can't stay here." I pushed past him.

"What?"

He opened his arms, both incredulous and welcoming.

"Sorry. No."

In front of me, I saw an old bed sunken to the floor; one French window opened onto a blank, concrete wall of the 21st century. When I walked over to the window, I looked down at a tumble of concrete blocks piled like bodies of suicides in an alley below.

"This is awful," I said.

"Jen, goddamn it," he said affectionately. "Give me a kiss hello."

I turned and kissed him quickly, noting the bedspread's sickening yellowish hue. "I can't stay here."

He put his hands on my shoulders. "Look at me."

"I can't. I want to leave right now."

"I paid already."

"I know. But it's putrid. Look." I pointed to the bed.

"Kiss me," he said again.

"How can you in this place?"

Other items clicked through my head: No lace canopy. No poofy quilt. Where were the pleated lamp-shades? Two pillows lay in flimsy cases. I spotted a rip in the duvet.

"Raoul. It's torn. See that? Let's go." I nodded to the depression in the bed, at the leftover outline of sleepers, confirming my doubts. I turned to the door.

He crossed his arms, immovable.

"You're tired," he said. "Did you sleep on the plane?" His

dark eyes, full of endless expressions, searched mine for clues.

"I took an achievement test for success."

He laughed and took a step. "Hun. Put your bag down. We'll look for something else tomorrow. It's early," he said, checking his watch. "We'll get some breakfast, come back and sleep. Tomorrow we'll go somewhere else. You'll feel much better. There are hundreds of hotels in Paris. This isn't the greatest but it's not that bad. We're in Paris."

"You don't understand." I sat down on the single chair against the wall, ready to combat my heart's minutiae. "I had a completely different vision. Hotel Liszt. It was the music. The famous name fooled me. It's my fault. Why did they call it Hotel Liszt? It's insulting."

"For people like you. It's a gimmick. So what?"

I pulled open my overnight bag, squirmed my fingers between bunches of cotton clothes, and found the hard corners of the guidebook.

I read aloud. *"Charming, restored Victorian in what was once the fashionable Opera district tucked away* – blah, blah – what crap. What lies! *Once* – hear that? *Was.* Get it?" I tossed the book on the bed. "I wasn't paying attention."

"You're exaggerating. Come on. Listen to yourself." He stood in front of me.

"Some Paris," I said, noticing his thighs in his jeans. I leaned toward him and wrapped my arms around his waist. Everything about him felt built to last. I pressed my face into his front zipper.

I nudged my forehead between his legs and thought about alternatives. I was tired, overcome with the idea of having to move, depressed by waves of the room's ugliness and my disappointment. I opened my eyes. "Some

Liszt. It really is an affront to call it that. For that reason alone we should leave."

He took my hand. "It's got nothing to do with reason. It's economics. If we leave now we won't get our money back. Neither one of us is rich."

"We're not poor and I hate that kind of excuse." I leaned away from him. I didn't want to be reduced to money. I hadn't come here for that.

"The shower's new, see?" He urged me up. "We'll take a shower. You'll feel better. Come on."

Raoul's optimism and drive stemmed from his immigrant roots. He knew how to reinvent his landscape. If something wasn't working, he made a plan to better it. His parents, Cuban Jews, fled to Miami when he was three. His father worked multiple jobs, eventually bought a small bungalow on *Calle Hocho*, the Cuban section of Miami, and opened a hardware store. If Raoul insisted on staying in this hellish place, perhaps I was missing something.

I walked into the bathroom and admitted the sink looked modern. Even the wall tiles looked new. He helped ease off my skirt and blouse, underwear and bra. He undressed, too.

"Don't put them on the floor!" I cried. I reached for my clothes and piled them into the sink, then tiptoed into the shower stall.

"Maybe it's a girl boy thing," I said. "This sorry decor. It's upsetting."

He turned up the hot water and adjusted the dials. "Forget the hotel. You're here. I'm here. Right? That's what counts."

He smoothed his hands along my hips and I relaxed into his chest. The warm water flowed down through my toes, then rose in a pool around my ankles; the shower basin was filling up. This set me off again. "See? The drain's not working. I must be blind," I said, "falling for a place like this. I'm leaving. We have to. This is ridiculous."

"Right. So stop."

But I leapt out and swiped a rag of terry cloth down my sides. Then I tiptoed to my suitcase, put on clean socks and jeans, and walked over to the 21st century wall again. It was more gray than white, reflecting an uncertain future.

"Now you are driving me crazy," he called from the bathroom. I heard him turn the shower off. He came out and put on another pair of jeans and a raspberry-colored shirt, my favorite. A cool Easterly wind blew in from Hungary, or so I imagined. He shut the window.

"What's the matter here? It's you and me in one of the most famous towns on earth. What else do you want? Let's get to the bottom of this."

"Maybe you're here because of Paris, not me. I don't understand what I'm doing with my life."

"Oh, oh, oh, oh, oh," he said, gallantly swinging his arms into the air.

This, I knew, signified his near breaking point. But the thing about Raoul, even in his sternest moments, he forgave me.

"Maybe I am here for Paris *and*," he said, clasping his hands, "I love you."

This silenced me. We had talked about liking, wanting, needing each other, but now this word, *love*. I heard the elevator cranking. So it really works, I thought, distracted by that word. *Love*. Wanted it. Needed it. Scared of it.

I walked over to the suitcase and pulled out my soft, blue sweater thinking I had not been successful with previous lovers. There had been a pattern of attraction, sex, then the troubling commitment factor settling in like a dangerous weather pattern – reckless winds, torn branches.

I bent over and closed the bag. It took months for me to surface when Richard wanted out. Then there was Seth and a flurry of serial dating. Adam, the gynecologist. He wanted me but I coveted his beautiful kitchen, those straw-colored cupboards, sunlight stippling through his micro Venetian blinds, as if such tangible things could bring happiness, not mediocrity in bed – my mind traveling walls, awkward kisses; feeling numb.

All that, until I met Raoul.

Raoul was different.

I smiled, remembering.

"You look beautiful," he said to me.

"Oh," I said, tying up my hair, letting stray hairs fall any which way. Richard thought so, too, in the beginning. There was Kevin, the musical egotist, and that summer of one-nighters; and Seth, the confused college student who went overseas to study economics – he didn't talk about beauty; and another doctor who wanted to wrap things up – get his practice, house, future wife in order like polished medical reports. After Boston and Providence, I moved to Miami – geographic dislocation, environmental shift – to find something better than what I had.

"Darling," I said, taking two more steps across the room. "Admit it. It's ugly here. I just want to leave. Why don't you want to?"

"Why don't you want to stay?'

"I don't know." I shrugged and studied my socks but they had nothing to say. I looked at my feet lined up next to his. My socks faced the window, his feet faced the door. The window flapped apart and knocked against the wall.

From the start Raoul had a sense of humor, a lightness of heart. At the sales seminar he asked me to go for a run before dinner. We circled a worn track outside the convention center; he, mindless of the heat, the farting, the sweat-smeared strings of hair plastered to my forehead. Our first kiss tasted of salt, ice cubes and lemonade.

"WHAT ARE YOU thinking?" he finally said.

I took a longer look at the room. "Everything, I guess. I had this idea that everything would be spacious." Seeing the armoire for the first time, I went over and opened it. Inside a yellow blanket hung from a hook. I smelled dusty odors, like old, lonely thoughts. A plastic bag for laundry lay folded on a shelf, never to be used.

"Come on. Jen. Stop. It's been two weeks – ."

"I know." I stepped closer to him. "Two weeks is too long. That's the problem. It's too long and I'm tired."

"I'm tired, too."

He held my arms and leaned back on the bed. I fell on top of him and rested my chin on his chest. Another gust of wind curled and rippled the curtains back into themselves.

"I get it now. This happens every time," he said, flipping his head back to look at the curtains flailing.

"What do you mean?"

"Every time we haven't seen each other, you go through this. You give me a hard time."

He held me and we rested for a while without saying anything. When I opened my eyes again, I saw the coffin, which was really the armoire, but at that point everything looked moribund. His chest rose and fell in silent rhythms. I pushed away lint on his shirt and he awakened.

"Don't go to sleep," I said. "I want to stay, but not here. We'll sleep somewhere else. I'll call some hotels. Don't worry. I won't get fooled this time."

I spotted a phone book on a shelf next to the bed. "Look at that. Old Franz even has a set of yellow pages." This livened me up. I lifted myself off his chest and padded around the bed to the telephone. I closed the window again.

"The next one could be worse," he said without inflection.

"The next one could have a recording of Beethoven." I laughed sadly. "Who knows what that'll do to me? Maybe you should call."

"I'm not calling anyone."

"I'll call the Ritz. No surprises there. " I picked up the phone.

"You're out of your mind. We can hardly afford this." He sat up and looked around him.

"It's an ugly *this* and ugliness is never affordable," I said feeling determined again, hyper-focused on my darker turn of mind. "What's the price of a room when the immaterial costs are so high?" I started dialing. "Don't worry, I won't call the Ritz."

Instead, I called seven places. Every single hotel was full.

"That's it," he said. "What's going on here? Hand me the phone." He jumped over the invisible sleepers in the bed and took the phone from me. "It's early. Nobody's checked out yet. Talk to me," he said.

"Are you full?"

"No. I'm empty. You are wearing me out. Why are you doing this? I can't take much more. Look. It's after midnight our time, for chrissakes. We could have been sleeping by now. If we had been sleeping, half the time would have already passed. We would have been that much closer to tomorrow and by tomorrow we would have been long gone from here."

"That's true."

I thought about taking my clothes off again; then I saw the armoire that was really a simple pine box.

"I don't want to die here."

"You're making me crazy. Jesus. Seriously. What's going on with you?"

He sat up and waited.

"It's hard to keep separating. I'm tired of it," I finally said as if I knew this all along but was terrified to admit it. "We spend all our days apart. I spend more time visiting you in my dreams. All week I'm awake and you're not with me. You could be dead for all I know. All week I live with a memory of you. I wonder about myself. What's wrong with me? All my kisses go to Chili, my dog. I have conversations with a pregnant lawyer woman and her urologist husband. I hardly know them, yet they know what time I go to bed and what's wrong with my car. They go to the places I shop. But to you, my daily life is a fossil, a description. I'm beat. I'm getting too old for this."

"That's two of us."

I shook my head, expecting the worst, not quite hearing him. Richard didn't want to be needed. Seth didn't care. Benjamin hoped for a perfect match to his perfectly planned life, not imperfect me.

"Not just airplane tired," I said. "Tired of living a continent away from you." I looked at him in the yolky light, surprised by what I was releasing. "Sorry, but it's true." I dropped my head and waited for him to cut me loose; waited for the continental plates to crash and crumble this lovely togetherness we had started to form. I covered my face and cried.

"Don't," he said, stroking my hair, still damp from the shower. "I'm sick of it too. I love you. Why don't you move to California and live with me? Let's get married. Let's do it. It's time."

He touched my chin. "Sugar. How about it?"

I took his hands and we were silent, floating in a sacred circle of warmth like a wave of light coming over the hills.

"We can do this."

"Okay," I said. "Okay. Okay."

"Good. What else?" he asked. He caught a stray hair and smoothed it behind my ear.

"I want to have history with you."

He nodded. "We will over time. That's a given. Okay? " He kissed me and said, "Listen. We don't have to stay here. I'll say the shower isn't working. The drain's stopped up. We don't have to pay for what's not working."

"No. You're right. It's okay. It's just a room. One night. We can stay. I want to stay."

I slid my arm around his shoulder and nestled in, aligning his hips to mine, every part of him touching me now. A surge of compassion for this run down hotel changed how I saw things. The armoire – just a humble structure pressed in the most dignified way into a corner. It didn't deserve my blame. How many discouraging conversations had it listened to? How many fights?

Sheets soiled, towels rubbed to threads? This room had history. A life. Outside, that pitiful wall didn't ask to be here, either. I appreciated its dilemma: banished to an alleyway without light, doing its best to give us privacy in this luminous city, where lovers traveled skyward for thousands of miles to reach a truer understanding of their fate.